By Jody Feldman

Illustrations by Victoria Jamieson

 Greenwillow Books

An Imprint of HarperCollins *Publishers*

The Gollywhopper Games
Text copyright © 2008 by Jody Feldman
Illustrations copyright © 2008 by Victoria Jamieson
Jacket photograph copyright © 2008 by Philip J. Brittan/Getty Images

The text of this book is set in Caslon.
Book design by Victoria Jamieson

Library of Congress Cataloging-in-Publication Data
Feldman, Jody.
The Gollywhopper Games / by Jody Feldman;
illustrations by Victoria Jamieson.
p. cm.
"Greenwillow Books."
Summary: Twelve-year-old Gil Goodson competes against thousands of other children at extraordinary puzzles, stunts, and more in hopes of a fresh start for his family, which has been ostracized since his father was falsely accused of embezzling from Golly Toy and Game Company.
ISBN 978-0-06-121450-9 (trade bdg.)
ISBN 978-0-06-121451-6 (lib. bdg.)
[1. Contests—Fiction. 2. Games—Fiction. 3. Puzzles—Fiction. 4. Conduct of life—Fiction. 5. Toy making—Fiction.]
I. Jamieson, Victoria, ill. II. Title.
PZ7.F3357752Gol 2008 [Fic]—dc22 2007021358

First Edition 10 9 8 7 6 5 4

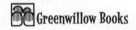 Greenwillow Books

To Dick, Paige & Cassie
and to my mom and dad
who worked to remove the rocks
from this long, long road

CHAPTER 1

If Gil Goodson was to have a chance, any chance at all, he would have to run faster than he was running right now.

Run. Away from University Stadium, packed with throngs of contestants who'd suddenly appeared from nowhere to get in line. Run, blinking back the sweat, pushing the lawn mower he wished he could abandon on the street. Run, past the lawn he'd just taken valuable time to cut because Mrs. Hempstead really believed the national TV networks might show her boring street. What were the chances of that happening? About as much as, as . . . as what?

As Gil had of winning the Gollywhopper Games?

One chance in 25,000—if he could still get a ticket. He'd been planning this day since last summer, ever since Golly Toy and Game Company announced the Gollywhopper Games.

With Gil's foolproof plan, he wouldn't have to buy zillions of toys and games to find one of 500 instant winner tickets. He wouldn't need to send in tons of entries, hoping his name might be drawn from millions and millions of others to win one of 20,000 tickets in that sweepstakes.

He lived eight blocks from University Stadium. He only needed to be one of the first 4,500 kids when the line opened at eleven A.M. today. The plan was to stand with his duffel and sleeping bag just outside the "no-enter" zone and storm the stadium at the front of the crowd.

He'd planned it all, except for yesterday's monsoon that had kept him from mowing Mrs. Hempstead's lawn. Why didn't he realize the mushy ground would keep him working for an extra hour? Why didn't he have weather ESP? Then he never would have let Mrs. Hempstead prepay him—double—to make her lawn perfect by this morning.

With the money already in the bank, Gil was stuck finishing the job. Only a thief would raise a son who took money then didn't do the work. Not true, but people might say that. Wasn't that one reason he needed to get into the Games? To erase it all?

Gil rammed the lawn mower into the splintered shed behind their pea-sized house, then jammed his key into the back-door lock. Inside, he grabbed a scrap of paper from the kitchen drawer and pulled out a pen. It slipped from his long, sweaty fingers and rolled under the stove. He grabbed another.

He raced to the front door, reached for the duffel, the sleeping bag and . . .

What was that smell?

It was him: a rising stench of grass and sweat and

lawn mower gas. Gil propelled himself down the hall, into the shower, beneath the cold water, fully dressed. He wedged off his shoes, peeled away his cutoff jeans, underwear, and T-shirt, and skipped the bar of soap over his body, squirted some shampoo on his wavy hair and urged the trickling water to rinse him faster. Then with one hand he turned off the shower and with the other grabbed the nearest towel. Damp. Who cared who used it last. His mom? His dad? He'd barely use it anyway. The August weather in Orchard Heights would finish the job.

He jumped into jeans that his legs had almost outgrown again, and by the time he'd struggled into a gray T-shirt, he was at the front door, hoisting the duffel over his shoulder and burrowing his fingers under the elastic bands that kept the sleeping bag rolled. He pushed his feet into his flip-flops, shoved a baseball cap on his head, and was back on the street.

Back toward University Stadium. Back past the parked cars bearing every license plate in the country. Back toward the massive line encircling the stadium then practically circling it again. Back past the horseshoe pits, barbecue grills, and volleyball games.

"Are you at the end?" he asked a man making camp with his kids.

"Not anymore, son."

Gil dropped his gear near a small tree and scanned the mass of bodies. How many of them were there? More than he could count. And no way he'd ask the reporter over there, take the chance she'd recognize him from The Incident.

Gil pivoted away, but seconds later felt a tap on his shoulder. Had she noticed him? He turned so the bill of his baseball cap masked his eyes.

Some shrimpy guy with a Golly badge handed him a yellow card. "Here."

"What's this?" Gil asked.

"It's not a ticket, but guard it with your life," said the guy. "If you lose it, you might as well go to the end of the line. The first person has number one, and you've got . . . Well, look at your own number. The first forty-five hundred have guaranteed tickets tomorrow morning, and I've heard maybe a thousand more will get in. Everything's printed on the back."

Gil looked at his yellow card.

#5915

5,915? No. No!

If he could somehow get in, even if 1,415 people who had instant win and mail-in tickets didn't show up, he still might be disqualified in the end. It was, after all, Golly Toy and Game Company that had had his father arrested.

Gil had flung open their front door after school on February 13, exactly eighteen months and two days ago, grumbling to his mom. Their teacher, who apparently lived in the Paleozoic Era, was forcing them to follow "the age-old ritual" of handing out valentines.

"Like we're supposed to learn something from shoving pieces of paper at each other. If they make us do this next year in sixth grade, Frankie and Lonnie and Donnie and the rest of the guys and I already decided. We're all gonna put worms in our envelopes."

Silence.

His mom leaned her full weight against the living room wall.

Gil's stomach moved to his throat. "What's wrong? Where's Dad?"

"He's okay," she said, "but he's at the police station, helping straighten out an incident at work. Someone tried to steal a lot of money."

"So why were you crying?"

"The people at Golly are like family." She took a shaky breath, cleared her throat, and straightened up. "Okay, then. Valentines, huh? Let's find something that won't embarrass you."

They spent the evening filling out valentines and playing chess, and the last thing Gil remembered was trying to stay awake through the end of an old Indiana Jones DVD.

The next morning, he rounded the corner for breakfast in time to catch his mom throwing away the unread newspaper. Strange. Both his parents always read it from first section to last, then re-cycled . . . Where was his dad?

Gil sneaked the paper from the trash.

Orchard Heights Times

VOL XVIIILI   "PICKED FRESH NEWS"   ONE DOLLAR

GOLLY EXECUTIVE ARRESTED, CHARGED WITH ATTEMPTED THEFT

The Goodson family in happier times.

ORCHARD HEIGHTS—Police yesterday arrested Charles Goodson, vice-president of Golly Toy and Game Company, for attempting to embezzle company funds. Goodson, 36, of Orchard Heights, was seized in his office at Golly and went peacefully with arresting officers.

A Golly spokesperson said the attempt involved an account theoretically accessible only to company president, Thaddeus G. "Bert" Golliwop Jr. and his attorneys. Goodson allegedly reprogrammed the computer system to send himself $25,000

each week until the fund, containing approxi-
mately $5 million, was depleted.

The company believes Goodson accessed the
account through an outdated series of passwords
once used to protect the files.

Goodson declared his innocence, but declined
further comment on advice of his counsel. A bail
hearing has been set for tomorrow morning.

That day at school, one group of kids bombarded Gil
with questions. Another avoided him like he was
a rabid bat. Even the whisperers outnumbered the
people who tried to treat Gil normally. Those reactions
weren't so bad, though, not compared to basketball
practice the next Sunday when Rocky Titus, this guy
in the grade above Gil, decided to slash Gil's arm
every time the coach wasn't looking. Even Gil didn't
see the last blow coming, the one that made him fall
to the ground, writhing in pain. He did hear Rocky
whisper, "Serves you right, you son of a crook."

By the time Gil's arm healed that spring, baseball
season had started without him. And when football
season began in late summer, just before sixth grade,

Gil thought he was ready to get back in there until Lonnie and Donnie, the twins in his grade, came up to him during their first practice.

"We've been thinking," Lonnie had said. "We don't want a cheater on our team."

"I'm not a cheater," said Gil.

"Yeah, right," said Donnie. "And your dad's not a thief. Go home."

Gil looked to his so-called friends for support, but they just shook their heads. That night, Gil convinced himself that sports weren't so great. Maybe he'd change his mind after the trial.

The trial that November was ten days of pure nastiness. Gil's mom had warned him that one whole set of lawyers didn't care about the truth. Their job was to get a guilty verdict and send Gil's dad to jail for a long time.

It was even uglier than that, but when the jury came in with a not-guilty verdict, Gil floated as if his body were filled with helium. Get ready, sports. Goodson's back!

"Wipe off that smirk," said Rocky Titus at school the next morning.

Gil felt all the color drain from his face. "What do you mean?"

"I mean your father's still guilty. They just couldn't prove it. Everyone knows that."

"You are such a jerk." Gil shoved past Rocky and tried to make himself invisible again.

After the trial, Gil's dad talked about leaving town and starting over, but even now, on August 11, they were still in Orchard Heights. His dad worked a low-paying job at the university library, then every night he'd comb through the investigation files the private detectives had left behind. Gil could barely get him outside to play catch anymore. His dad sat glued to the dining room table, scribbling in those old folders, typing into the computer. Again. And again.

"Are we ever going to leave?" Gil had asked his dad about six months ago.

He pointed to the files. "Can't afford to right now. Maybe soon."

"What if I can afford to?" said Gil. "What if I win the Gollywhopper Games?"

"You win," his dad had said, "and we'll move."

CHAPTER 3

"**H**eads up!"

A large toy airplane circled, landed three people away, and shook Gil from his memories.

He turned to take advantage of the gusting wind, then took a closer look at the yellow card that Shrimpy Guy had given him.

Ladies and Gentlemen!
Boys and Girls!
Welcome to the Biggest! Bravest! Boldest!
Competition of Action and Intellect
the World has ever seen!

Celebrating the 50th Anniversary of the
Golly Toy and Game Company!
Your number in line is: #5915.
Do not lose this Line Card!
It's your Chance for a Ticket to win Fame!
and Fortune!

The number on this card indicates your place
in line. You must hold on to your card or risk
forfeiting your right to receive a ticket
that might lead to winning:
*A full college scholarship!
*A copy of every toy and game Golly has
ever sold or ever will sell!
*Plus other stupendous prizes and experiences too
fabulous and too numerous to name!

Stick around. The ride of your life is about to begin!

The back side of the card said that even with this card, contestants must keep their places in line until tomorrow morning, when Golly officials would give further directions; that it was unlawful to sell or copy the card; the company was not liable for lost or stolen cards; the card came with no guarantees; and blah, blah, blah—all that small print to protect the company's backsides. Golly lawyers were good at that.

Gil sat against the tree, slipped his yellow line card halfway under his butt. He needed both hands to dig deep into his duffel for a bottle of water he'd packed yesterday. He took a long swig. Wiped his mouth with the back of his hand then wiped his hand on the duffel, right next to its stenciled letters. GILBERT.

Gilbert stunk as a first name, didn't have a cool nickname. Bert was the nerd on *Sesame Street* or the great uncle with hair sprouting out his nose and ears. And Gil? It wasn't spelled the same, but according to their disintegrating *American Heritage Dictionary*, it sounded the same as, "The respiratory organ of most aquatic animals that breathe underwater to obtain oxygen." Stenciled like this, though, Gilbert was the last name of his great-grandfather the military hero.

Gil took another gulp of water and tried to make himself believe that 1,415 kids with guaranteed tickets wouldn't show up. What about the kids from Hawaii or Alaska or even California or Connecticut? They couldn't all have parents willing to travel so far to play a game, no matter how exciting that game promised to be. Maybe he still had a good chance. Maybe—

"Duck!"

A ball from a volleyball game came like a shot toward Gil's head. He jerked and rolled over just in time. And just in time for one of those breezes to catch his yellow card and send it tumbling. He scrambled to his feet. Forget his water. Forget his stuff. His card, his chance to get into the Games, was cartwheeling backward, back toward the people who had worse numbers than he did. Gil couldn't go to the end of the

line. He just
couldn't. Run! Get
the card! Get—

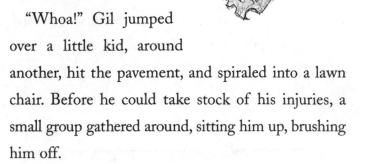

"Whoa!" Gil jumped
over a little kid, around
another, hit the pavement, and spiraled into a lawn
chair. Before he could take stock of his injuries, a
small group gathered around, sitting him up, brushing
him off.

"Are you all right, kid?" someone asked.

A woman rushed up to him with a first aid kit.

He tried to shake her off, tried to get back up. "My
card," he said. "My card blew away." He scrambled to
his feet and—

"Looking for this?" The voice belonged to a hand
that held Gil's card.

"Yeah. Thank you very, very . . ."

Oh, no. Not Lonnie. Not one of the twins. Gil
hoped they'd both flunked and had to stay behind in
sixth grade. Didn't matter right now. Lonnie stood
there, a Golly badge on his chest and a grin on his
face. If he and his brother were still identical, they'd
turned into twin giraffes over the summer. "How

much is the card worth to you?" he said.

"C'mon, Lonnie. Be decent for a change."

"Because your dad was decent at Golly? My dad still curses your dad every day because he can't remember all those passwords he needs to get into his computer stuff. They won't even let us kids preview computer games unless we go through forty thousand security checks. So for all my trouble, I think this should be worth something. If you want it badly enough."

The woman with the first aid kit stepped toward them. Her eyes came up only to Lonnie's chin, but she somehow appeared taller.

"Whose ticket is that?" she said.

"Why do you—"

The woman got right into Lonnie's face.

"I said—"

"Okay, okay." Lonnie handed Gil the ticket and walked away.

"Now sit yourself down," she said to Gil. "Nurse Francine doesn't want any back talk from you, either."

Gil wasn't about to argue with her. He sat. "My mom's a nurse, too."

"She's probably not a school nurse, though."

Gil laughed and let her tend to his knee through the rip in his jeans. "Thank you," Gil said. "For everything."

Francine helped him up. "Now you hold on to that ticket, you hear?"

Gil nodded, tried out his knee. It only stung a little bit. He raced back to his stuff, hoping it was still there. Hoping he still had a place in line.

CHAPTER 4

The wind had blown his sleeping bag a little, but all his gear was there. Gil took a deep breath, folded his yellow card, shoved it into the depths of his front pocket. He flopped down, looking toward the stadium, toward the masses in front of him, until a laugh shot out from behind him.

Gil turned and focused on long, white-blonde hair, then shocking pink fingernails.

The girl spun around, as if she knew his eyes were boring holes into her willowy shoulders.

He looked down. Picked at a thread on his duffel.

"Hi!" Gil heard her say. "Hello-o? Are you deaf?"

Gil looked up. "Who, me?"

"Yeah, you. I don't have eyes in the back of my head, so I'm usually talking to whoever I'm looking at. Maybe I'll call you Freckles."

Gil smiled.

"Or Dimples."

Gil smiled harder, scrambled to his feet.

"Anyway, hi! I'm Bianca LaBlanc. Do you like it? My name, I mean. My real name is BetsiJo Hammermeister, but have you ever heard of a super-model named BetsiJo Hammermeister? That's what I want to be: a model and an actress. Wouldn't it be great if I won?" She threw open her arms, gave a laugh. "They couldn't resist putting me in all their commercials. Me! BetsiJo Ham—I mean, Bianca LaBlanc. Anyway, do you like it? It means 'White

the White.' In two different languages. Italian and French, I think. I thought the name matched my hair. So? What do you think?"

Gil breathed her in, perfume and all. He wanted to ask if she ever took a breath when she talked, if she had always been this beautiful, and if that blond guy next to her was her boyfriend or her brother. Instead, he managed to say, "Yeah, I like your name. It's catchy."

"Oh, good. What's your name? You do have a name, don't you?"

"Gil."

"Just Gil? Like those famous people with one name?"

Gil laughed. "Gil Goodson."

"Hi, Gil Goodson. Double G. That's what I'll call you. This is my cousin Curt. He's twenty-one, way too old to do the Games, but he was at my house the night we found out my mom couldn't bring me here because of work, and my dad's off somewhere in New Mexico, and I started crying because I really wanted to be here to get discovered. So I promised Curt I'd pay for gas and give him ten percent of anything I won. And here we are! Right, Curt?"

Curt gave half a wave like he was used to Bianca grabbing all the attention.

Bianca adjusted her orange bikini top. "So what's your story?"

His story? Gil almost laughed, but he shrugged instead. "No story. Not really."

"You have to have a story. Everyone has a story, at least that's what Oprah said. I'm here to get famous." She pointed to the ABC camera. "They've already talked to me. So has Fox." She glanced over at the MTV camera. "They're next. So how old are you, Double G? I'm fifteen."

Twelve suddenly felt babyish. "I'll be thirteen soon." If three months was soon.

She looked him up and down. "Thirteen? That's all? You're almost tall as me. Great biceps. I would've thought you were closer to my age."

If the rims of Gil's ears burned any brighter, they'd glow like a neon sign.

"Anyway," she said, apparently oblivious to his ears, "we drove four hundred and eight miles just on the highway, and I'm so, so glad we're finally here."

Bianca stopped just long enough to breathe. "So, Gil," she said, "why are you alone?"

"My parents are coming after work," he said, practically drooling over the thought of the food they'd bring. He'd forgotten to eat breakfast. "Do you know what time it is?"

Bianca held up her wrist. "My watch is somewhere in my suitcase in the car. I didn't want to get a tan line. But Curt has a watch. Curtie!"

Curt had drifted toward a few guys farther back in line. He motioned Bianca over.

"Hold on. I'll go find out," she said.

When it looked like she'd planted herself with Curt near the MTV camera, Gil decided to chance leaving his stuff for just three minutes to get a slice of pizza and a soda. If he died of starvation, he couldn't play anyway. He reached into his back pocket to pull out his mon—

What? Who robbed— No. The money was in his shorts in the bathtub. He couldn't run home and leave the line for that long. He'd have to distract himself until his parents came. Which, looking at the sun, was more than four hours away.

He unrolled his sleeping bag, then watched the Goodyear blimp cruise overhead. It reminded him of that one Golly picnic when he was about seven. After dinner they'd had miniblimps circling the park grounds, occasionally dropping toys from their underbellies. All the kids chased them around for hours, until a parade of waiters carried out cakes that seemed to shoot fireworks from the icing.

And that was just a usual Golly picnic, so what would fifty years of celebration be like? How Gil wanted to know! He couldn't sit still anymore. He got up. Jumped. Jiggled his arms, waggled his head, just in time for Curt and Bianca to come back and see.

She looked at Gil like he was nuts. "Don't go spastic on me."

"I'm just nervous about getting in," he said. "I want to know."

Bianca grabbed his hand. "C'mon, Double G. Curt'll watch our stuff. Won't you, Curtie?"

"Sure."

Bianca pulled Gil behind her. "Let's see if we can find out how many people with real tickets haven't registered yet."

They stopped and watched an NBC person interview a kid.

"Why are we watching this?" asked Gil.

"We're not," she said. "We're waiting for the TV people. See what they know."

Gil knew one thing. He wasn't comfortable in media land. Didn't want to be spotted by the local stations. Didn't want them to bother him about the past.

Gil darted his attention all around, ready to make a quick getaway if someone should come storming up to him. A glint of steel from a wheelchair blinded him for a second. Gil blinked. Was that who he thought it was? "I'll be back, Bianca," he said. "He might know."

"Who? That old guy?"

"Yeah. Old Man Golliwop. Stay here."

Bianca, apparently, didn't listen because she was right behind Gil, weaving around people and chairs and tents until they were walking alongside the wheelchair.

The old man kept cruising, chuckling like he'd just remembered the funniest joke he'd ever heard.

"Well, isn't this something, Young Goodson?" he said. "Isn't this something? Hoo-boy! I hope you're playing in my games. I hope you take that dang loony son of mine for every nickel he's handing out. You are playing?"

"If I can get in," said Gil. "Do you know how many people they're taking from this line?"

"Nobody at my company tells me anything anymore. They think I should shrivel up and go away." Old Man Golliwop turned to Bianca. "Are you playing, too? Or are you one of those girls from TV?"

"I wish," said Bianca.

"You should be on TV. Next time you see me, Young Goodson, remind me to tell Bert he needs to hire her. But don't get your hopes up, young lady. My son won't listen to me. He didn't listen to me about your father, Young Goodson. Went on with that foolhardy trial."

"Yes, sir," said Gil, sorry he came up to the old man. "We need to—"

Old Man Golliwop aimed his wheelchair at Gil and stopped. "Remember when I practically ran my wheelchair over a dozen people to see what happened at the end of the trial, Young Goodson? I had a lot to say, and I still remember every word. Ha!"

Gil liked this story, but didn't need Bianca to hear every word. "I think—"

"Yessiree. Remember, Young Goodson? I told Bert that any fool could see he'd been wasting time and money trying to hang the wrong fellow. And that he had better get his facts straight if he wanted to keep running my company." Old Man Golliwop shook his head.

"Do you remember what my own son said to me?" He didn't wait for Gil to answer. "He said, 'It's not your company anymore, Dad.' And I reminded him I started my company with a nickel and an idea, so if I wanted to call it my company, I could dang well call it my company."

He grabbed Gil's wrist and looked him in the eye. "Then he wouldn't give your father his job back."

Gil shook his head. "My dad said he didn't want it back, remember?"

"Waste of talent. Waste of talent."

Gil glanced at Bianca. Hoped she'd been side-tracked by another TV camera. Or at least that the conversation had confused her. It didn't look that way, though. "Well, sir," said Gil, "we need to go."

"Yes you do. I don't want anyone to think I'm sharing company secrets with you. But before you leave, you need to promise me something. Promise me I'll see you at headquarters on Saturday. Promise."

"I can only try."

"That's as good as a promise." Old Man Golliwop reached up and thumped Gil's back. "Attaboy!" Then he wheeled off.

"And exactly who was that old guy?" Bianca asked.

"He started all this," Gil said. "Fifty years ago today."

"You mean the Games?"

"No, the company. That's Old Man Golliwop. Thaddeus G. Golliwop, founder of Golly Toy and Game Company."

"And he actually knows you? Personally?" Her green eyes were open wide. "You do have a story. Spill."

Gil started walking. "It's old stuff. Boring."

"Didn't sound boring." Bianca reeled ahead and blocked Gil's path. "Details. Now."

"It was nothing," he lied. "Someone accused my dad of trying to steal money from Golly, but he was found not guilty. And he didn't do it. That's all."

"Then what . . ." Bianca pointed behind Gil. "Ooh. Game Show Network! Let's go."

Gil let her drag him from one camera to the next until he'd had enough. He found his way back to the tree. Plopped onto his sleeping bag. Lay down. Sighed. If only . . .

CHAPTER 5

"**G**il. Gil! GIL! You alive?"

Gil bolted upright. People. Grass. Tree. "Huh?"

"Hey," said Frankie, one of those head-shakers from football practice.

In his haze Gil pictured Frankie diving into the pool at the house that should have been Gil's. The house—south of town, with a media room off the den and a bathtub so big you could swim in it—was nearly finished right before The Incident. Gil's parents had been grateful that Frankie's bought it from them so quickly, but every time Gil saw Frankie, he also saw the zipline that should have been his own. And he couldn't forget that day at football practice.

Gil gave Frankie a nod, and Frankie apparently took it as an invitation to sit on the sleeping bag. "I saw you sleeping here a couple hours ago, and when I came back, you hadn't moved a muscle. I was checking to make sure you weren't dead."

"Wishful thinking?"

"Crud no." Frankie brushed his dark hair away from his eyes. "Why'd you think that?"

"Football practice last year. The twins practically kicked me off the team. You shook your head and walked away."

"Because they were jerks, and I couldn't believe what they were saying."

"I thought . . ."

"You thought I wanted you off the team?" Frankie shook his head. "I was hoping you'd come back. My mom said you probably would if I gave you a little time. And I've tried the time thing, but today I decided this has been ridiculous."

"Huh?"

"You're never anywhere anymore. Not football or baseball. Not even at lunch during school last year. Where'd you eat? The bathroom?"

"Gross, Frankie." And it was, the one time he'd tried it. "I ate in the science room."

"Which could be gross, too."

"Not if you avoid the rabbit droppings." Gil smiled again, wondering why this felt so easy.

"So now that I found you," said Frankie, "I've gotta tell you, football league practice starts next week, and we need a wide receiver. You were the best."

Gil dug at some dirt underneath his fingernails. "Rocky was always the best."

"Rocky was always a jerk. Probably still is, but he's long gone. You know that."

Gil snapped his head up.

"You didn't notice he was gone? Man. You have been a hermit. If you believe Rocky, his dad got this perfect new job a bunch of time ago in Maine or Wyoming."

"How can you confuse Maine with Wyoming?" Gil laughed.

"Don't care enough to remember. Anyway, the dad left first, and when he got settled in some mansion, Rocky and his mom moved there, too." Frankie groaned to a stand. "But I don't want to

talk about him anymore. Gotta get back to work."
He pointed to his yellow Golly badge. "Can you
believe they're actually paying employees' kids to
hang around in case people have questions? Have
any questions?"

"No. Thanks."

"Okay. Football field. Next week. Be there."
Frankie turned and walked away.

Gil's gut said to stop Frankie and ask what day,
what time, what field. Ask if the twin giraffes would
be there. And whose side the other guys were on.
Instead he watched Frankie disappear behind the hot
dog smoke billowing from a grill.

Food. Gil needed food. He reached into his duffel,
hoping to pull out an eight-course meal, but he came
up with his three Golly notebooks instead. Those
notebooks had been his sport for the last six months.
After he made that deal with his dad, Gil started
collecting every shred of information he could find
about Golly, then studied the company like another
subject.

He opened Volume 1 for the millionth and maybe
last time.

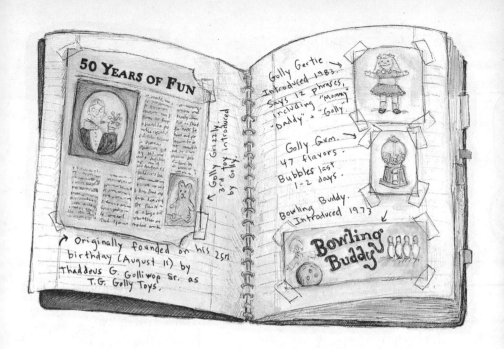

Originally founded on his 25th birthday (August 11) by Thaddeus G. Golliwop Sr. as T. G. Golly Toys.

Exactly fifty years ago today. Should have wished the old man a happy birthday. He flipped to page three.

In the first year, introduced one new product each month. Now the largest company of its kind in the world with more than 800 toys and games on its active sales list, including cutting-edge video and computer technology.

After a while, he found himself reading page ten for the fifteenth time, not because it was complicated but because he was distracted from it by whiffs of barbecued chicken and popcorn and now, pepperoni pizza so close he could almost—

"Here."

Touch it?

Frankie was back, holding two slices and a humongous soda for him. "Thought you could use this. Don't want our wide receiver wasting away in line."

Gil smiled, but didn't reach for it.

"C'mon. Take it. One of the side benefits of this job. We get all the food we can eat."

"Seriously?" Gil didn't want charity. "My money's at home in the bathtub—don't ask—but I'll pay you back."

"Now there's an idea," said Frankie. "Get free food and sell it. We could . . . Wow! Wow-wow! Of all the perfect dreams. Don't turn now, but way over there, there's this girl—"

"And she's wearing an orange bikini top and unzipped jean shorts covering her bottoms, and she's heading right for us."

"You psychic, Gil?"

"Yeah. Call me Magno the Magnificent." Gil

smiled. "No. Her name's Bianca. She's my next-door neighbor here. She's fifteen, so stop drooling."

"I can dream, can't I?" Frankie pulled his attention away from her. "Gotta go, but I will return." He looked over his shoulder three times before he was out of sight.

"I'm back, everyone," Bianca said, "but I'm not too happy." She flopped onto a lounge chair next to Curt's. "I couldn't find out anything."

Gil took a bite of pizza and slapped Volume 1 closed.

Bianca pointed to the notebook. "Whatcha doing?" she asked. "School stuff? It'd be a crime if you were one of those people who study before school starts. Those, those yolk-heads."

"It's eggheads, Bianca," said Curt.

"Whatever." She leaned over and grabbed Volume 1. "So what is this?"

Gil explained the notebooks.

Bianca read a chunk of the history, flipped through the stock market pages, then lingered on the newspaper articles that interviewed some of the instant winners. "Wow! Gil!" she said. "I didn't know we'd have to know anything. I just thought . . . I don't know what I thought I'd have to do. Hey, Double G, I'm gonna stick with you. Mind?"

Gil shrugged. "Watch my stuff?" He got up to use one of the Porta Potties. Yeah, he did mind. He'd been clever enough to figure out what to do. He'd made and studied the notebooks. He'd worked all sorts of puzzles his dad had copied and brought home from the library. But he didn't need to make another enemy.

He went back to his spot, trying not to look mad, and when he saw two water bottles and some Laffy Taffy ropes in the shape of an *F*, he actually smiled. Frankie had struck again.

Gil took a bite of candy and sat there. Saw Bianca crack open Volume 2 of the notebooks.

"It's like watching paint dry," said Curt. "C'mon, Gil, let's go play volleyball."

And risk someone else kicking him off another sports team?

"C'mon, Gil. Bianca will watch our stuff."

He got up. Why not? The twins were working. Most other kids from school would be, too, if they were even here. Their parents still had jobs at Golly. Lucky them.

In spite of everything, Gil missed going to Golly headquarters on Saturdays with his dad. He remembered one particular morning when he was nine. They'd opened the door to his dad's office and there, sitting like a person at the desk, was a life-sized bear, pretending to type at the keyboard. The screen invited Gil to come to the testing room and bring his friend. Using the bear as a chair, Gil spent hours testing a huge loop-de-loop car track that collapsed into a carrying case without needing to break down into a million pieces. He wanted to take that home so badly. He wondered why Golly never did make it. It was amazing.

So was the volleyball they were playing with. Gil didn't know if Golly sold this one yet or if they were watching today to see how it tested out. It was regulation white, until you hit it. Then depending on the spot, it glowed a different color. He couldn't wait to see it at night.

Gil got into the game fast. Set. Set. Spike. Dig. Set. Spike. Score! The rhythm of the game seemed as natural as breathing. He did miss sports. Even as hot as it was, he didn't want to take the rotation out, especially because both Lonnie and Donnie were on the sidelines waiting for him.

"Now what?" said Gil.

"Lonnie told me you were here," said Donnie.

"And?" Gil said, putting on his best I-dare-you face.

"And nothing. Just didn't believe you existed any-more." He looked at his brother. "He's still got game. Shouldn't be here, though."

Lonnie shook his head. "You know you shouldn't be here, Gil."

"I checked the rules," Gil said. "None of my relatives

have worked at Golly for more than a year. I'm eligible."

Lonnie shrugged. "They should've added a Goodson rule, you creep. Let's go, Donnie."

Gil felt sorry for the volleyball. Knew he'd smash the air out of it the next time it came his way. Set. Set. Spike it right at the twins. Score.

Would this always be his life in Orchard Heights?

CHAPTER 6

The announcement came over a loudspeaker at 8:30 the next morning. "Ladies and gentlemen! Boys and girls! It's Gollywhopper Day! All contestants and their guardians must be in line in five minutes. A team of Golly representatives will lead you to a designated registration area where we will issue the remaining tickets."

Gil jumped up. "This is it," he said to his parents.

His mom and dad had shown up early yesterday evening with carryout fried chicken—enough to share with Curt and Bianca—and for the rest of the night they ate, sat, talked, stared at the stars, listened to music, and watched the line grow longer and longer. Somewhere between two A.M. and dawn, Gil managed to doze off. Right now, though, he was too nervous to be tired.

He rolled up his sleeping bag, and by the time he retied his duffel, a group of Golly workers was walking toward them. The Golly people led their section of the line to an enormous red-and-yellow banner over a long bank of tables with ten more workers stationed behind.

Line Cards #5501–#6500
REGISTER HERE!

"All right," came a voice over a bullhorn. "Please take a place in any of the ten lines here. No need to push. Our computers will scan your cards and tell us if we're accepting your number yet. Just have your yellow line cards ready. We have room for some of you."

"How many?" Bianca shouted.

"How many?" came the echoes that went unanswered.

Gil wound up deep in one line with Bianca right next to him. An Orchard Heights High School cheerleader handed them each a registration form and Gollywhopper Games pen. "Fill this out before you get to the table."

It didn't take long to reach the front of the line. "Good morning," said the woman behind the table. "Your yellow cards and registration forms, please."

Gil and Bianca passed their cards and papers to her as if they were a team.

The woman scanned the cards under a weird light. "We want to make sure you didn't set up a little counterfeiting operation last night," she said with a lilt in her voice.

Gil knew she was trying to be funny, but . . .

A light flashed green.

"We're in?" Gil asked.

"You're in."

"We're in!" Bianca grabbed Gil's wrists, and they jumped in circles.

Gil hugged his mom, his dad. Bianca hugged Curt.

The woman handed each of them a set of rules, a souvenir ticket, and a numbered square, like the kind Olympic runners wear. "Stick these on, then go over to Security. If you have any electronics, cell phones, PDAs, or other illegal items, you can check them there and retrieve them when you leave the stadium. About ten feet beyond that, we have room to store your camping equipment. Good luck!"

"That's my cue to leave," said Gil's mom. "Call me at work when you get home." She hugged Gil's dad, then ruffled Gil's hair before she kissed him on top of his head. "Go get 'em," she said, then made a face. "That was lame."

"Yeah, it was," said Gil.

"How 'bout, try your best? Have fun? Think hard? Crush, kill, destroy?"

"Don't take any wooden nickels," Gil said.

"Look both ways before you cross the street," said his mom.

"Chew before you swallow."

"Don't run with scissors," his mom called, walking away with all their stuff.

Once they passed through Security, Gil and his dad and Bianca and Curt settled on a bench near the twenty-yard line, and not a minute later, the university band marched in. With the band providing background noise, Gil read the instructions four times. If he understood them right, this part of the competition would be great for his legs that itched to run.

Too soon, the band headed for the sidelines, but before the last marchers left the field, they yanked away some tarps covering a center stage. Underneath were microphones, amps, guitars, and drums. Four guys in jeans and T-shirts streaked onto the field. One more strutted after them.

A couple people screamed. More and more did, too.

"Do you know who that is?" Bianca jumped onto the bench. "I love you, Skorch!"

The music started hard and loud with Skorch's number one hit. A guy in front of Gil spun around. "If I lose," he said, "I don't really care now. I got to see the hottest concert in the world without paying for a ticket."

Gil and Bianca and almost everyone else sang at the top of their lungs and jumped and danced to each of Skorch's songs until he played his final number and ran off.

Instantly four men in neon green Golly vests took their places around the stage, precisely spaced as the

four main compass points. Simultaneously each grabbed the end of an upright roll of orange plastic construction fencing that had been secured to the field. Then each man marched straight ahead, toward the seats, up through aisles, pulling the netting and clamping it to posts every four rows until they reached the very top. They came down, raced back onto the field, and staked four immense banners to the ground, labeling one section A, one B, then C and D.

The stadium clock hit ten seconds, creating a contagious countdown.

"Three! Two! One!"

On cue, a booming voice resonated over the loudspeaker. "Ladies and gentlemen. Boys and girls. It's what the world's been waiting for. The Golly! Whopper! Games! Are you ready?"

CHAPTER 7

"Please!" the announcer boomed for the fourth time. "Ladies and gentlemen! Boys and girls! Please!"

The shrieks and whoops began to fade.

"I'm Randy Wright, your voice of the Gollywhopper Games, the ultimate competition, celebrating Golly's fifty years in the fun-making business. So let's make some fun!"

The crowd cheered again.

"I know! I know! You're excited to get this party started, but first, important instructions.

"Your rule sheet tells you this portion of the Gollywhopper Games consists of multiple choice questions. As I read the questions, they will appear on the scoreboard. Look up there now.

"If we were to ask, for example: Which company is sponsoring this great event? A. Terrific; B. Gosh; C. Super; or D. Golly, your number one toy and game company in the entire world, you would all pick answer D, but how will you show your answer? Notice. The stadium is divided into four separate sections, each designated A, B, C, or D. When we've given the signal, you may get out of your seats, go into the concession area, and follow the arrows around the stadium, clockwise—that's to your right—until you get to the section that matches your answer.

"We guarantee you will have enough time to find a place in your chosen section. For everyone's safety (and this is vitally important): Do not run. Do not push. Do not climb over the nets. Do not go the wrong way. And always remain with your adult. Violators will be eliminated on the spot.

"Also, adults. This is a competition for your eleven- to fifteen-year-olds. You must not help the contestants in any way."

"Yeah," said Gil. "How many adults won't help?"

"At least one," said his dad.

"Good." Gil was suddenly glad Bianca and Curt were along for his ride. They could be witnesses in case someone accused him of cheating.

"When the concession area is nearly clear," Randy continued, "we will start a five-minute countdown before the final buzzer. Then we will announce the correct answer. If you are in the right section, remain there. If you've chosen incorrectly, please find the nearest stadium exit. On your way out, you will receive a ten-dollar gift certificate toward the purchase of any Golly product plus a free copy of Skorch's new CD.

"Good luck, contestants. And now . . . the moment you've all been waiting for. Let the Gollywhopper Games begin!

"Question! Number! One! How many letters plus punctuation marks are in Golly Toy and Game Company's first advertising slogan?

"A. 27; B. 28; C. 29; D. 30.

"Okay . . . GO!"

Most kids lunged for the aisles.

"Where are we going?" asked Bianca.

"I can't exactly go anywhere until I figure it out," Gil said. It wasn't the slogan that slowed him down. Golly still printed it on every package. Gil counted the letters on his fingers once, then twice. Twenty-five, both times. Now for punctuation.

The slogan always came with a balloon-style exclamation point. Twenty-six. Still not enough letters and marks to match any of the answers. Gil took his new Golly pen from his pocket. On the instruction sheet he scribbled: *If it's fun it's by Golly, by golly!*

One comma? Yeah. Gil was sure. Twenty-seven. Okay, okay. Section A. Wait. The apostrophes! "I say section C." Gil handed the paper to Bianca. "Double-check my numbers."

She counted, then stood. "Let's go."

The four of them wormed their way up the aisle. Gil had to believe it'd be easier to move down five seats and jump the net than go three-fourths of the way around the stadium, but when they stepped inside the concession area, it wasn't the mess he expected. It was more like an orderly game of musical chairs.

They fell into step, passed the rest of section D, all of A and B, then entered the sunlit areas of section C with two minutes to go. Clambering over the feet and knees of a dozen people who had already hogged the spaces hugging the aisles, Gil moved down to the netting separating C from D. The backs of his legs were a millisecond from hitting the bench when Bianca grabbed him by the shoulder and whirled him around to face her.

"Are you sure about the answer? Absolutely, positively, down-to-your-very-soul sure? If we got the very first question wrong, I think I'd crumple up and die."

"Yuck," said Gil.

"No, really."

"Really, Bianca? If I thought I was wrong, I'd be racing like a wild man. Instead, I'm going to sit on this nice, hot bench."

"Then why are more people over there?" Bianca pointed toward an overflowing section B.

Were they right? Had Gil imagined the comma? Was there really an exclamation point?

Buzz!

Gil jumped. Too late to move now.

"If," Randy's voice boomed, "you'll cast your attention to the scoreboards, the wrong answers will disappear, one by one, until only the correct answer remains. Hit it!"

The crowd rose. Wild cheers thundered. All four answers on the scoreboard flashed off and on, flickering faster and faster. The board went black then lit back up with answer A, gone.

Groans rose from that section.

The flashing began again. Answer D, gone. It was down to B and . . .

"Ahh!" Some kid had scrambled under the flexible fencing, banging into Gil's ankles, toppling Gil onto his dad. "Security!" screamed Gil, but his voice tumbled into the cheers from his section because only answer C remained.

The nearest guard, two rows below, was staring forward. The one three rows above was tending to some man who had a cut on his head. Gil looked for another—

But his dad grabbed him from behind and lifted him up and down. Bianca gave him a hug. Curt whacked him on the back.

The cheater and his adult were leaping, slapping high fives, blending in. Guiltless. The kid turned to Gil for a high five.

Gil blinked and looked again. Shuddered.

The kid did a double take. He pointed at Gil. "Hey!" He laughed. "If it isn't the son of a crook!" It was Rocky Titus.

"And you're talking because you're Honest Abe?"

Rocky puffed his chest. "Prove I'm not."

Gil couldn't. "Just go away."

"We already did. Left this boring town for the big city." Rocky grinned. "You should see our new house. Huge pool. Floor-to-ceiling TVs. Video games like you wouldn't believe." He elbowed Gil. "You still living in that ugly house?"

"It's better than your face." Gil turned his back to Rocky and watched his own dad talk to Mr. Titus.

Gil had always thought Rocky's parents were nice people, so it never made sense that their son was the biggest creep in the Midwest. Now that Mr. Titus had cheated right alongside Rocky, Gil was beginning to understand.

"So," Rocky whispered into Gil's ear, "maybe you're worth following. Did your old man steal the answers before they arrested him?"

Gil stared at the scoreboard, felt his toes clench and release the soles of his flip-flops, tried to forget the jerk was here. Impossible. So he stared some more, jittered his knees, waited to start playing again.

Finally Randy's voice reverberated over the speakers. "Question number two! Golly's very first board game—like many Golly games since—depended on a roll of the dice to keep the game moving. Using that first game as a clue, when were dice widely believed to have been invented? At the same time as:

"A. The presence of the Shang Dynasty—before 1000 B.C.; B. The expansion of the Roman Empire—around 257 B.C.; C. The age of knights during the Middle Ages—around 1010 A.D.; or D. The cultural movement of the Renaissance— around 1410 A.D."

What was Gil supposed to be, a walking encyclopedia? He looked at his dad and shrugged. His dad shrugged back. So did Curt.

"I wish I knew," Bianca said. "I really want to help."

Gil smiled at her, but he doubted it.

"Where to, Gil?" said his dad.

"You know this one, don't you?"

His dad's expression didn't change.

All those facts Gil had studied, all that information about business structure, stock options, insurance providers—that all meant nothing if he couldn't figure out when dice were invented.

He looked at the question again. "Using Golly's

first game as a clue," Gil said, reasoning out loud. "Okay. Their first game was The Incredible Treasures of King Tut and—"

"King Tut?" said Bianca. "I know him. What do you want to know?"

"You're kidding, right?" said Gil.

"I'm crazy about him, Double G. He was the kid king who ruled for nine years and had more gold and jewels than, than . . . Well, he just had tons. They buried him with it. Cool and gruesome. Ask me anything."

"Do you know when he died?" said Gil.

"Not exactly . . ."

Gil's stomach sank.

"But I know he was born like in thirteen forty B.C., because thirteen forty is my locker number at school. That's how I remember history. You gotta love history. So he must've died—"

Gil grabbed Bianca's hand and pulled her into the aisle. "You can follow me anywhere," he said.

She beamed. "I did good?"

"You did great."

Inside the concession area, Gil didn't need to look

back to feel Rocky lurking behind. He wanted to turn around and slug the guy, but Gil just walked harder and faster and tried to feel lucky that he'd still be in the Games after answers B, C, and D disappeared. And when the scoreboard finally started flashing, C was gone! D, gone! Then . . .

B? The right answer was B? No!

The section next to them cheered.

Gil sank to his knees and pounded the bench in front of him.

Rocky screamed something obscene.

Bianca sobbed on Curt's shoulder. "I know history. I really do."

Gil's dad put a hand on his back. "I would've been wrong, too, but . . . No. You're right. They're—"

"HOLD ON!" Randy's voice pierced through Gil's gut. "No one leave!"

The people around Gil stopped as if caught in a freeze-frame.

"We've had a malfunction. The scoreboard has the wrong answer. The wrong answer!"

The scoreboard went black. Gil held his breath and closed his eyes until he heard the crazy cheers from the contestants surrounding him.

"Sorry for the mix-up, folks," Randy said. "The correct answer is now on the board. Those of you in section A, please remain where you are. To those of you in other sections, we apologize for the mix-up and ask you to exit quickly. You'll receive an autographed copy of Skorch's CD and a twenty-dollar Golly gift certificate."

Gil's breath came in gulps. He put his head in his hands and wished he could go home, sleep for a while, and come back tonight. But he was here, and most kids were gone.

"Hey, Gil," Bianca said a few moments later.

He came back into daylight. Blinked to adjust his eyes.

Bianca was pointing about ten rows below them. "Isn't that the guy from your notebook? I don't recognize his adult—I can't remember why you even had a picture of him with his dad—but I'd know those red cheeks anywhere."

Gil stood on the bench to get a better look. "Yeah. It's Thorn, the rich kid. He bought about five thousand Golly toys and games before he found an

**Billionaire spends $100,000
on Golly toys to secure ticket**

Houston, TX:

instant winner ticket. And that guy with him looks
more like a bodyguard than his—Huh?" A wad of
paper bounced off the top of Gil's head and hit
Bianca's shoulder.

They both turned. Rocky was grinning at them
from three rows up.

Gil grabbed the wad and opened it. How appropriate. "He threw the rules away."

Bianca turned and stepped up on the bench behind them. "You jerk! You could've hit someone in the eye."

Rocky started laughing like it was the most hysterical thing he'd ever heard.

Bianca took another step up. Curt grabbed her arm and . . .

Gil had had enough of the drama. He just wanted to keep playing. Looked around. Tried to estimate the number of other kids he needed to beat. "How many still here, Dad? Four thousand?"

"Fewer," said his dad. "If you—"

"Congratulations!" Randy announced. "By our calculations, there are between twenty-five hundred and three thousand contestants remaining."

That answered that.

"So congratulate yourself for making it into the top ten to fifteen percent." Randy paused for the crowd's rumble, then continued. "You have two more questions to answer today. For the final question, we'll do something different, but for the next one, we'll stick to the same multiple choice format. And here it is!

"When Thaddeus G. Golliwop founded Golly Toy and Game Company, he was the same age as Charles Lindbergh when Lindy made the first solo flight across the Atlantic Ocean. Give us that age.

"A. 25; B. 27; C. 29; or D. 31."

Without wasting a second, Gil stood to leave for the concession area. He looked back. His dad's eyes wouldn't meet his.

Gil smiled at him anyway. "Don't worry," he said. "Don't worry."

With his dad, Bianca, Curt, Rocky, and Mr. Titus in a parade behind him, Gil made a giant circle around the concession area until he led them back to section A.

"You do know where we are, don't you?" asked Curt.

"Isn't this where we just came from?" said Bianca. Gil's dad smiled.

"Sorry," said Gil. "Needed to move."

His plan to shake Rocky hadn't worked. Not that he'd expected it to. Maybe soon. Maybe . . .

Dozens of workers were racing onto the field, placing small desks onto the turf in haphazard rows. Maybe for the next question, Rocky couldn't follow him.

Gil watched. He waited. And when the scoreboard started flashing, he held his breath, hoping he hadn't made a mistake, hoping he could—

"A!"

Gil jumped. He screamed. He hugged his dad. Wanted to call his mom and tell her he'd beat Golly at least a little. It wouldn't pay to gloat. Not now, though. Not yet. Not unless he made it through the final elimination round of the day.

CHAPTER 8

Gil thought he might explode. He'd just inhaled two hot dogs, a bag of peanuts, a slice of pizza, and some cotton candy, all washed down with a giant root beer. When he'd first gotten into the food line, he didn't think he'd be able to eat a thing. But if Golly was giving away free food, he was taking it.

Right now, though, he volunteered to make a trash run. He needed to stand and give the food space to spread out. Back in the concession area, he turned to the left, against all the arrows from the previous game, and started a lap around the stadium.

He was tempted to pick up more peanuts and a few candy bars to take home. That stuff was expensive.

Would it make him a thief, though? Probably not, but he'd live without it.

He'd made it to the next round. He'd get at least as much as the last group to leave—a fifty-dollar Golly gift certificate plus an autographed Skorch CD—but now he wanted the whole pizza. He wanted the prizes and the victory. He wanted Bert Golliwop to look him in the eye and shake his hand. He wanted to give his dad the opportunity to return to Golly headquarters tomorrow, for the first time in eighteen months, with his head held high.

Mostly he wanted a fresh start, to move to Phoenix near his aunt Katherine. Or to St. Louis, where his parents had met at college. Only a win could guarantee him enough money for that. Gil wished he'd made a different deal with his dad. Gil could've said, "If I get into a second round, we'll move. Deal?" But no. He needed to win.

Gil grabbed a bottle of water and headed back to his seat. Sidled through the row. Sat.

"You look tense," said his dad.

"A lot of pressure."

"Only if you want it. Nothing will change if

you win or lose. Nothing important, that is."

Did his dad forget their deal? Or was he being philosophical? Gil took a hard gulp.

His dad looked at him. "You okay?"

"Yeah. Just . . ." Gil hesitated. "Just wondering how many contestants are left," he said. "I'm thinking eight hundred forty-two."

"No. Last round eliminated more folks than that. They probably didn't think someone so young could start such a huge company."

"So how many?" said Gil.

"Wild guess? Five hundred fifty," said his dad. "Go beat 'em all."

As if on cue, the buzzer sounded.

"Ladies and gentlemen . . ." Randy boomed. "Please direct your attention to the desks on the field. Each is identical. No desk will give you an advantage over another. I invite you to make your way to one of these desks. Adults, please accompany your contestant to a seat then return to the stands as this portion of the Gollywhopper Games continues."

Gil turned to Bianca. "Doubt I can help you here. Doubt you can help me. This may be it."

"Hey," she said, flashing him a huge smile, "we got this far, didn't we?"

They walked toward the football field, where desks stood in rows, spaced two yards apart, spanning the width of the turf. They all faced the stage in the center. Gil spotted a desk on the thirty-two yard line between two that were already occupied. He took that one on purpose.

To his left sat a spindly boy with glasses. To his right sat a girl whose face looked about fourteen but whose black ponytail and pink ribbon belonged on a preschooler. Perfect. No distractions.

He looked up at his dad and smiled. "I'm good."

"I'll be in our old seats. Remember? Thirty yard line, west side?" Gil's dad put a hand on Gil's shoulder.

"Gotcha."

Before his dad could leave, the mother of the ponytail girl marched up to Gil's desk. "Excuse me," she said. "I couldn't help but overhear. You seem to know exactly where you're going after this, young man."

"Yeah?"

"This stadium is so large, I'm afraid I'll lose Lavinia in the crowd. If I sit near your guardian, would you lead Lavinia back?"

"Sure. No problem." Gil glanced over at Lavinia, expected her to be under her desk from embarrassment. But she sat there like she was used to this. Then he looked at her hands. She was gripping them together so hard her knuckles turned white.

"Very well," said the woman. "I'm Mrs. Plodder. And your name?"

"Gil."

She looked at him like she expected more.

He stood. "Pleased to meet you. I'm Gil Goodson. This is my father, Charles Goodson."

"Pleasure," she said. "If you'll give me one minute." She went back to Lavinia's desk. "Are you sure you're all right here, dear?" she said.

"I'm fine."

"At least they had bottled water. You never know about water in these small towns. Remember what happened when you attended that scholars competition?"

"I'm fine, Mother."

Gil shook his head. Did she think they got their water straight from the creek?

"All right. Do remember to follow this nice young man afterward."

We're really ax murderers, Gil wanted to say.

"His name is Gil."

"Yes, Mother. I heard."

Mrs. Plodder turned to go off the field, and

Lavinia looked over at Gil with her large, brown eyes. *Sorry,* she mouthed.

"No problem." Gil smiled, and that smile eased his shoulders until Randy's voice blared again.

"Congratulations on making it to the last stop in today's competition. Please pay particular attention to these instructions," said Randy. "On your desks, you have a pen, a pad of paper, and a gadget that looks like a calculator. We call this your keypad.

"First, look at the number on your shirt. That's your contestant number. Punch that exact number into your keypad, then press the enter key."

Gil pulled out his shirt and rechecked to make sure the number still said 24682. He punched it in, looked up, and had to laugh. Some of the other contestants were contorting their shoulders, craning their necks, almost turning their heads upside down to read their numbers.

The announcer continued. "Now, get ready for the question. *The* question. Your answer to this question, one question only, will send ten of you into the greatest, grandest competition we could conceive: the ultimate final rounds of the Gollywhopper Games.

"Your answer will be a whole number. You may use the pen and paper on your desks to calculate your answer. You may not use the keypad. It will not work as a calculator. It will only record your answer and transmit it to our computers. So punch in only your answer. Carefully. Once you've pressed *enter*, your answer has been recorded, and you may not change it. You will have ten minutes to accomplish this task. When time is up, your keypads will lock automatically.

"Our computers will determine the ten contestants closest to the correct answer. In the event of any ties, the winning spots will go to the contestants who entered their answers first.

"For this part of the Gollywhopper Games, you may not receive help from anyone. Do not stand up. Do not kneel on your chair. Remain silent. Any violation of these rules will result in immediate disqualification.

"The question will remain on the scoreboard for the full ten minutes. Here it comes.

"Add:

the number of instant winner tickets that were available for the Games,

the number of squares on a checkerboard,

the date in August Golly opened for business,

the number of people going to St. Ives,

the number of contestants now remaining,

the number of spots on a pair of dice, *then*

"Multiply: that total by the number of different toys and games Golly introduced in its first year of business."

Gil's heart pumped so loudly he couldn't hear himself think. His mind went blank. Don't panic now. Settle down. Breathe.

He stared at the question. Add. Multiply. This was math. He was great at math. One, two, three, four, five, six. Six questions to answer, six numbers to add together. Then one more question to answer, and one multiplication problem to work. One step at a time . . .

The number of instant winner tickets.

Easy. He wrote, "500."

Squares on a checkerboard.

Same as a chessboard, but he'd never stopped to count the squares. He'd count now. How many pieces spanned its width? Forget the pawns that all look alike. On the bottom row: two rooks, two knights, two bishops, one king, one queen. They took up eight spaces, times eight going the other way. He wrote, "64."

The date in August Golly opened for business.

August 11, yesterday, on Old Man Golliwop's birthday. Should've wished him happy birthday.

Whoa, Goodson. Stay focused. He wrote, "11."

The number of people going to St. Ives.

Where was St. Ives, and who gave a flying fart anyway? St. Ives, St. Ives and lives. No, wives. The old nursery rhyme. Did he even remember that? Yeah, he did. He stared at a nick in the desk and ran the rhyme through his mind.

As I was going to St. Ives,
I met a man with seven wives.
Every wife had seven sacks,
Every sack had seven cats,
Every cat had seven kits.

Kits, cats, sacks, and wives,

How many were going to St. Ives?

Seven wives times seven sacks: forty-nine. Times seven cats . . . Wait. No. *They* weren't going to St. Ives. *I* was the only one going to St. Ives. Gil wrote down "1."

The number of contestants now remaining.

He couldn't have studied for that, but he could do some figuring. One hundred yards on a football field. Desks spaced every two yards. That was fifty rows. No, fifty-one. He had to include both end zones. But wait. Rows spilled beyond the two end zones, too. Ten yards per end zone for maybe ten more total rows, plus four more in each end zone past that. Now, how many desks in each row? Gil looked up and straight ahead, trying to make it clear he wasn't cheating. The row several ahead of him held sixteen desks, but the row ahead of that had fifteen. And then there were the incomplete rows on either side of the main stage. About a thousand desks, minus the ones that were empty.

What now? What should he put down? He'd guessed eight hundred forty-two. His dad, five hundred fifty. Which one? His dad had been closer before, but would it be cheating to use his number? Doubtful. It's not like they knew that their guesses would be part of the Games, but Gil didn't want to take a chance. Only one way to go. He added the two numbers and divided by two. Then he wrote his answer. "696."

The number of spots on a pair of dice.

Too easy. He wrote "42" on his paper.

He added the six numbers. He added them again and a third time, then wrote, "1,314" on a clean piece of paper. Time for the final part.

The number of different toys and games Golly introduced in its first year of business.

How many? This was the most important question of all, the multiplier.

Gil closed his eyes and mentally opened the first notebook. Page three, at the bottom. He'd read those words a million times. "In the first year, introduced one new product each month."

Gil set up the equation, did his multiplication three times, then punched the number into his keypad. 15768. *Enter.*

He leaned back and allowed the tiniest smile to

brush his lips. He knew the exact answer for each question except one. And no one knew that answer unless . . .

Why did Rocky keep darting his head toward the stands?

Mr. Titus was there, moving his stare along the desks at the far end of the field. He turned his head straight forward, whipped out a pen and paper and scribbled something. Then he rubbed his nose and touched his chin and pulled his ear like baseball managers do when they flash signals to their players. He stopped and nodded.

Rocky entered an answer into his keypad then reclined in his desk chair, crossing his arms over his chest like he had just finished Thanksgiving dinner.

Gil couldn't look at Rocky anymore. He shifted his gaze away.

About eight yards up, that rich kid, Thorn, was digging a finger in his ear. Gross. But it was like looking at roadkill. Gil couldn't tear his eyes away. Instead of a sticky ball of wax, Thorn removed a flesh-colored blob. A hearing aid? So the rich kid wasn't perfect. Thorn examined the earpiece, flicked it twice then replaced it in his ear. Wait a minute! Who needed a hearing aid to think?

All Gil could do was laugh or else he'd scream. Here he was, worried about borrowing some random number from his dad and those two . . .

Forget them. He still had a chance. A good one.

A couple minutes later, the keypads went dead; the microphone came alive. "Please stay seated and silent," said Randy. "We'll be back to you in a matter of minutes."

That's all the time it took. Bert Golliwop strode to center stage, holding an envelope and a microphone.

"I'm Bert Golliwop, your host for the Gollywhopper Games, and . . ."

"Stop the happy talk," Gil said under his breath. "Say something important."

"Inside this envelope," Mr. Golliwop said, as if reading Gil's mind, "are the numbers of the semi-finalists, the ten who came closest to our number: 15,900."

Gil did some quick figuring. Missed it by only 132. That had to be close enough. Had to.

"We will call contestant numbers starting with the

closest to the correct answer. If I call the number on your shirt, please join me on the stage."

"Come on. Say my number. Two forty-six eighty-two. Say it," said Gil under his breath.

"Here goes."

"Say it. Two forty-six eighty-two. Say it."

"Number one seven eight two seven."

Some guy from the other side of the field shouted and bounded onto the stage.

"Number zero-zero-zero-zero one."

Big surprise. Thorn ambled up, like his mom called him to dinner. And he wasn't hungry.

"Number zero three seven oh two."

A short boy came from behind him. The kid looked eight years old.

"Number one eight six four three."

Rocky's father figured it right. Rocky galloped up with fists punching the air.

"Number one zero zero three five."

A shriek came from somewhere. Man, that girl was cute.

"Number two four six eight three."

One off! Who . . . Bianca? How did she make it?

Gil almost fell off his chair.

"Number zero nine four three one."

The genius girl with the overprotective mom.

"Number two four six eight two."

Bingo! Gil didn't remember getting to his feet and didn't know how he got to the stage. All he knew was he was up there. He did it. HE DID IT!

Gil found himself turning in circles, shaking hands, hugging Bianca, getting hugs from the other girls, back-patting Rocky, not caring that he was such a cheater. He high-fived a brown-haired girl and a guy with curly hair who followed him up there.

Curly Guy started making a beeline for Bianca, but a man in a green vest stopped him. Another green-vested person herded Gil and Bianca to seats behind a long table on one side of the stage next to Thorn, Rocky, and Genius Girl. The remaining five contestants sat at a table on the other side of the stage.

Bert Golliwop thanked everyone still at their desks and instructed them to pick up a signed Skorch CD and one hundred dollars in cash as they exited.

One hundred dollars? That would probably mean nothing to Thorn, but if Gil could come away with one hundred dollars in cash? Jackpot!

Mr. Golliwop addressed the wave of reporters and TV cameras that rolled toward the stage. "Let me introduce you to our survivors." From the cards in his hand, he read off the names of the five kids to his right. "And to my left, Thornton Dewitt-Formey, Rocky Titus, Lavinia Plodder, Bianca LaBlanc, and . . ." He quick-turned his head at Gil then turned back. "Gil Goodson," he said, his voice a half note higher.

"Excuse me," he said, picking up a glass of water. "I think I may have swallowed a bug."

A few people laughed, but Gil just smiled.

Mr. Golliwop cleared his throat. "All right now. We'll take fifteen minutes for questions from the press, then let these kids go. It's been a long day." Bert Golliwop's stare zeroed in on a local reporter who had been particularly nasty to Gil's family in the past. "And, please, ask general questions that can and will be answered by all our contestants."

The local reporter gave a slight nod back. "How

old are each of you?" he yelled out.

Bert Golliwop exhaled before he cleared his throat. "We'll begin with the young lady to my far right."

All ten answered. Lights shone in their eyes, TV cameras pointed toward their faces, and photographers clicked away. The questions came fast and furious.

"Where do you live?"

"Describe your feelings in one word."

"Do you think you'll get any sleep tonight?"

"What will you do if you win it all?"

Gil fell into step, hoping the questions would remain easy, and they did.

When the press conference ended, Mr. Golliwop came from behind his podium and faced the ten of them. "Those of you who don't already have hotel accommodations in town, please see my assistant over there. We'll make arrangements. Also see her if you need extra tickets for additional family members. And try to get a good night's sleep. You need to be at Golly headquarters tomorrow morning by nine o'clock, with parent or guardian, and dressed comfortably for competition." He looked at Bianca's shoes. "You might want to rethink those high heels, young lady."

Bianca laughed.

"Now I want each of you to look at the others at your table. The five of you need to become best friends because you're now a team, and you'll be competing against the other five. That's all I can tell you. Before you leave, take a minute and introduce yourselves."

They stood and formed a little circle, but Gil didn't listen to the introductions. Instead he studied his team.

Bianca. Bianca was great. Bianca made him smile. And maybe she knew more than it seemed. Somehow she'd made it on stage.

Lavinia was the biggest question mark. Gil hoped her mother was cautious because she wanted to protect a genius-sized brain and not because she was a six-year-old in disguise.

Rocky looked even stronger than he used to be. Great if there were physical challenges, but the team needed to stop him from cheating or they'd all risk elimination.

Thorn? Ditto on the cheating.

The cheating. Gil had to do something about the cheating. He'd tell someone, but who would believe him? Bianca might. Or Bianca might yell, reporters might come running, and Gil might have to answer thousands of questions. He'd figure out something by tomorrow.

Gil got an extra ticket for his mom, then walked toward the stands with Bianca and Lavinia. "Okay, Bianca," he said. "How'd you figure out that last question?"

"It was easy," she said. "I mean, it was hard. I figured out most of it and came up with fourteen thousand something, but the number didn't feel lucky, so I went with some luckier numbers. I used my age today: fifteen. Then eight because my birthday's in eight days, plus sixteen because that's how old I'll be. Fifteen thousand eight hundred sixteen. Get it?"

Gil shook his head. Maybe Bianca was smarter than he thought. At least her luck was beyond belief. If only it would hold out through tomorrow and rub off on him. If only . . .

Gil saw something shining where the field met

the track. "A lucky penny," he said. If only it were lucky enough to get him out of this cheating mess. It wasn't so much Rocky who concerned him. He could probably handle Rocky. He didn't know about Thorn.

Gil reached for the penny, fumbled it between his sweaty fingers, and it pinged against the track. He picked it up again and smiled.

Yeah. Now he could deal with Thorn.

CHAPTER 9

Gil stopped cold, then backed behind a bank of bushes near the top of their street. He gestured with his chin.

"Ah. TV trucks," Gil's dad said. "Should've known."

Gil should've known, too. Reporters always come back. They'd camped outside Gil's house for a week after the arrest. They returned during the trial. They stayed after the verdict until other news moved them to a different location.

At first, they acted so nice, like they were trying to get the Goodsons' side of the story. It turned out, though, they wanted to be heroes and find the one piece of evidence that would prove his dad guilty. Now they were back in force today, but with their national media buddies.

"Well," said his dad, "we have three choices. We call the police and issue a nuisance complaint, which will give us bad press again. We sneak around Jonathan Street and try to slip inside the back door unnoticed, but we already know that won't work. Or . . ."

"Yeah," said Gil. "Let's do the 'or.'"

"I think our official line is no comment," said his dad. "That's always safest. Ready?"

The media swarmed toward them like a wave of gnats, flapping their cameras, recorders, notepads, and flashes.

"How can you be eligible?"

"How'd you know the answers?"

"Is this revenge?"

Gil kept his eyes on his target: the front door. If he could make it through, smiling and silent, he'd win this round.

Gil's dad put an arm around his shoulders. Together they strode onto their lawn and up the two

porch steps. Instead of turning his key in the lock, Gil's dad turned and faced the crowd.

"I've been silent for eighteen months," he said. "And I'd prefer to remain that way, but when you ask insinuating questions of a twelve-year-old boy, I can't, as a father, remain silent. So all I will say is this. See this strong, young man who stands in front of you? He wants only one thing today and tomorrow. He wants to find some joy in life by playing a game. Playing a game. It's as simple as that. So please leave him alone when he eats tonight. Leave him alone to sleep. And tomorrow morning, let him play, just as you'd want your own children to do. Now, good evening." He turned, opened the door, and shuttled Gil inside.

"You shouldn't have, Dad," Gil said. "They'll put it on the news and in the—"

His dad shook his head. "You didn't notice, did you?" He nudged open a corner of the living room curtain. "Bert Golliwop's limo. See? Behind the Channel Four news truck? This isn't the publicity he wants. I guarantee."

Bert Golliwop, flanked on one side by a police

officer and on the other by a woman in a suit, cut through the reporters and up to the Goodsons' front stoop.

Gil's dad opened the door to let them in. "Bert," he said. "Coming to arrest me again?"

Mr. Golliwop let out a fake laugh. "No, Charles, no. I'm trying to quiet this little situation."

"Be my guest," said Gil's dad. "But why the police?"

"Me coming into a semifinalist's house? Don't want to give an air of impropriety. Officer Lane is here as a witness. So is Samantha Phillips from the commission that oversees rules and procedures."

"Officer Lane, Ms. Phillips, I respect your positions," said Gil's dad. "So please don't take this as an attack on your integrity, but I feel the need to call in a couple witnesses of my own."

"Who do you have in mind?" asked Bert.

Charles Goodson opened the front door. "Excuse me," he called to the reporters. "Claire Dawson? Mike Owens? Are you there?"

Reporters from the *Orchard Heights Times* and the Channel 5 News came forward.

"Dad?" said Gil. "But those two—"

"They were the fair ones. Tough, but fair." He motioned them inside, told them why they were there, and asked them to turn on their recorders. "Now please, Bert, you were saying?"

"I was saying that I came as a courtesy to quiet the situation on the street. That's all. I'm afraid you've wasted the reporters' time."

"Don't worry about our time," said Mike Owens. "Now, off the record, Bert. Awkward situation, the son of a fired executive in the round of ten. Any comment?"

Bert Golliwop stared at the reporters. "Off the record? Turn those recorders off."

They did.

"Off the record, I have a multibillion dollar corporation to run and shareholders to consider. Any leader of any company would have nightmares from a situation like this." Bert Golliwop pointed at Gil. "I wish he weren't in the Gollywhopper Games. I don't think it sounds right. I don't think it smells right. I don't think it looks right even if the officials say it's all right. It's not. It's all wrong." He looked at

Gil's dad. "How much did you help your kid inside the stadium?"

"He didn't help me at all," said Gil. "And I have my own two witnesses to prove it."

"Gil, it's okay," said his dad.

"No. I have three more witnesses." Gil raced to his room, grabbed his notebooks and ran back, holding them high. "These are mine. I spent six months putting them together by myself. I memorized everything inside, just ask me. Your company discontinued five products last year including the Ping-Pong line. When GolTagaCo opened on the stock market, it sold for six dollars a share. What else? You, Mr. Golliwop, were born on August twenty-third, twelve days after the company opened for business, and the *G* of your middle name stands for Gilbert, which didn't excite me when I found out. You want more?" He thrust the notebooks toward Mr. Golliwop. "I worked hard to get here, maybe harder than any kid in that stadium. I wouldn't take anything I didn't earn. Neither would my dad, and if you think you can go around accusing—"

"Gil," said his dad.

"Hold on," said Bert Golliwop. "I'm not taking you to court over this, son."

Son? So many words tried to race from Gil's mouth that they stumbled over his tongue and struck him silent.

"I simply want you to know, Gil, we have ten alternate contestants for the Gollywhopper Games. Except for the one winner, all of them will receive the same prizes. If you don't want this heat, you can trade your spot with an alternate and collect your parting gifts."

Gil opened his mouth to speak.

"Before you answer," said Mr. Golliwop, "also understand that if you stay, you'll have more TV cameras and microphones pointed at you than all the other kids combined, and there's nothing I can do about that. It could be very uncomfortable. Think about it, son. It may be in your family's best interest if you relinquished your spot."

"I understand everything," said Gil. "See you tomorrow."

"Very well." Bert Golliwop nodded, opened the door and walked directly toward the reporters, who began shouting questions at him. He held up his hands and brought his palms down, quieting them. "I was inside, talking to one of our contestants, assuring him he'll be treated no differently than any other. So if you plan to retain your press passes for tomorrow and for any future Golly event, you'd be wise to pack up immediately and stay at least three blocks away. And people, keep your focus on the Gollywhopper Games, not on ancient history."

CHAPTER 10

"I'm playing a game. I'm playing a game. I'm playing a game," Gil kept whispering to himself the next morning. No different than chess or darts or tag.

It's just a game, he had said over and over to himself in bed last night when his brain kept nagging him for missing his chance to tell Bert Golliwop about the real cheaters. He didn't remember sleeping, but here, in the bathroom, his mouth tasted like he'd licked lawn mower dirt.

Gil loaded his toothbrush, pushed it around his mouth, and glanced down. His shoes were double-knotted. His socks matched. His fly was zipped. He spit and rinsed and reached into his right pocket to make sure the penny he had found yesterday was still there.

Just a game. He moved to the kitchen and grabbed a handful of Lucky Charms cereal then dug out and ate as many extra horseshoes and four-leaf clovers as he could find. Gil stuck his mouth under the faucet and gulped some water.

Just a game. He took a pair of scissors from the drawer and pulled the left front pocket of his jeans inside out. He snipped a couple stitches, stuffed his pocket back in and wedged two fingertips into the new hole to stretch it. "Sorry, Mom," he whispered. "It's part of the game."

Gil ran his fingers through his hair and exhaled. Looked out the window. No reporters today. He was ready.

He and his mom and dad spent the ten-minute drive to Golly headquarters in silence. His parents didn't try to start conversation, and Gil couldn't think of a thing to say. It all seemed petty compared to what his dad, in particular, must be feeling.

This was the first time Charles Goodson would

step into Golly since the day he was wrenched out in handcuffs. He never even got the chance to clean out his office. The police had seized everything, including Gil's kindergarten artwork that had decorated the walls for years.

The car climbed the hill that would give them the first view of the biggest building in Orchard Heights. Gil had been down this road dozens of times since The Incident, but the sight of the eight-story structure with its jumble of architecture—castle spires, modern angles, village awnings—shimmied up his spine like shock waves from an explosion.

They dropped Gil's mom off at the front entrance as specified on her ticket then swung around to the parking lot. A guard stopped the car, verified they belonged, then directed them around traffic cones painted like candy corn to an area of the lot reserved only for contestants.

"What time is it?" said Gil.

"We still have fifteen minutes." His dad turned off the engine, but made no move to get out of the car.

Gil stared at the building, too.

"I've been trying to think of something brilliant to say," said his dad. "Something to make the past year and a half disappear and allow you to go inside without all the garbage."

"It's okay, Dad."

"But I'm a dad, and dads have to say something." He shook his head. "The past few months, I'm afraid I've been too busy to say much of anything."

"It's okay," Gil said again.

His dad gripped the steering wheel and shook his head. "No. It's not. So I've been trying to think of something very philosophical, but my mind keeps returning to football." He swiveled in his seat to face Gil and almost smiled. "You know when we watch a game and the referee makes a rotten call, and the people on the sidelines stamp their feet and throw their helmets and drop their clipboards?"

Gil nodded. "And you can see the squiggly veins on the sides of their heads popping out?"

"You got the picture. Now, the players on that team have two choices. They can let the call rattle them and blow the rest of the game, or they can channel their indignation into energy and action, and use it to work harder."

"And that's what you want me to do."

His dad shook his head. "No. You've already done that, Gil. You prepared, and you played smart. Already, you accomplished more than I could have dreamed. And the fact that we can enter this building with our heads held high means we've already won. We have nothing left to prove. So throw away the garbage, and play that game. Don't let anyone drain the joy away from you. Just have fun." His dad grabbed Gil's hand, gave it a squeeze. "Ready?"

Gil nodded.

He felt ready for something. A firing squad? A pack of wild dogs? An ejector pad to launch him through the roof after he stepped inside the rainbow-striped door?

He was closest with the wild dogs. Hundreds of miniature windup toys barked and quacked and rattled around the entrance to the building. Gil tiptoed over and around them, careful not to step on the clown-faced rhino or the chattering teeth. And

when he knocked over the duck-billed chimp, it promptly righted itself and turned three circles before it clattered away.

Just the promise of coming here used to make Gil laugh. Around every corner, there'd always be balloons or life-sized stuffed animals or action projections of Golly's newest video games. And when he'd stop and breathe in, his nose could always detect a faint smell of chocolate-chip cookies or popcorn or apple pie or other scents that made him drool.

Gil's dad sniffed. "Fresh-baked bread today."

Gil nodded. "How do they do that?"

"I never wanted to know," his dad said. "I was afraid it'd shatter the fantasy."

The fantasy. The building was like one big fantasy.

Gil and his dad followed blinking arrows on the wall that led them through a narrow passage and into the biggest fantasy room of all: The Kaleidoscope. It wasn't a handheld toy, but an entire circular room that rose the full eight stories, walls glittering with a mosaic of shimmering, shining glass panels more brilliant than Gil's senses could take in.

He couldn't resist standing on the eight-pointed golden star in the room's center. Arms extended, face toward the sparkling ceiling, he twirled until the kaleidoscope's glass seemed to revolve around him. Then he stopped and wobbled. Let his knees buckle. Landed flat on his back, with the kaleidoscope spinning even faster.

His dad laughed.

"You told me to have fun."

"So I did."

Gil pulled himself up and regained his bearings. "Where do we go now?"

"Good morning, Gil." The angelic voice rolled across every pane of glass.

Gil looked all around but saw no one.

"Welcome to the Gollywhopper Games," the voice said. "Please continue through the appropriate door."

There were eight. The one straight ahead, however, pulsed with a golden glow. Behind that door, another room with its muted blue walls and fluffy-cloud ceiling made Gil feel almost as if he were standing in the middle of the sky. Two hot-air balloons hovered at the top, suspending a welcome banner. Underneath sat five wooden footlockers, rounded like pirate treasure chests.

Gil's dad shook his head. "You can't hate this place," he said.

Gil went over to the trunk with his name engraved on top. Dangling above, a poster-sized purple envelope read,

Lavinia's was the only envelope already opened. Gil tugged his loose from the kelly green ribbon suspending it from the ceiling. He reached in and pulled out the yellow paper.

Dear Gil,

Once upon a time, a long, long time ago, there was . . . STOP!

Wait. Cease. Desist. Fast forward. Here. Now.

No more past. No more future.

Concentrate. Here. Now.

Plug in your brain. Rev up your mind. Stretch out your legs.

This may be the most amazing day you'll experience. Ever.

A whirlwind of sights.

An explosion of sounds.

A feast for your senses.

All wrapped in a tangle of games.

You've already won everything inside this trunk, including some items dating back to once upon a time. Exactly what? You'll have to wait.

DO NOT OPEN THE TRUNK NOW. There will be a time and a place and a purpose for everything. Remember that.

Best of luck,
Golly Toy and Game Company

P.S. Leave the letter and envelope here, and follow the blinking green arrows.

"What green arrows?"

His father pointed down.

"Right," said Gil. "Because if you're looking for blinking arrows, you expect to find them sunk into the floor."

Gil read the letter once more, trying to memorize it for any clues he might need later. Then, with his dad beside him, he followed the green arrows to the right, down hallways lined with framed documents, signed and stamped with gold seals. Seals as in animals.

They ended at a green door, guarded by a redheaded woman dressed in jeans and a green shirt. "Gil, you're here!" she said like a long-lost friend. "I'm Carol. Nice to meet you both. Gil, when you're ready, go right in and wait for the rest of your team. And Mr. Goodson, stay put for a sec. We'll show you to the spectator area, a luxury section above the action. Perfect view."

His dad gave Gil a firm squeeze around his shoulders. "So long," he said.

"See ya," Gil replied.

"Adios."

"Aloha."

"Shalom."

Gil turned toward the door, which opened by itself. "Sayonara." He took a last glance over his shoulder and stepped inside. On a shining wooden floor stood a massive wooden table surrounded by sixteen burgundy leather chairs. An imposing bookcase guarded the corner. It was all serious and businesslike. The rest of the room, though, was lit like a giant party. Balloons bobbed, masking every inch of the ceiling. Fun house mirrors saluted like soldiers on either side of a second door. Giant streamers and noisemakers popped out of vases like flowers. Murals of kids, animals, cartoon characters, food, and toys splashed the walls.

It took Gil a moment to realize Lavinia was already there, looking very small in one of those chairs. Her hair was gathered in a turquoise ribbon and her intertwined fingers gripped one another on top of the table.

"Hi," Gil said. "You look as nervous as I am."

Lavinia shrugged. "I keep trying to fool myself that this is like any other scholarship competition, but the gorilla rocking chair over here makes that hard to remember."

"So does this guy." Gil popped the bounce-back wrestler in the gut a few times.

"Like Mother says, if we keep our focus, we should win." Lavinia gave a sharp nod like she was trying to convince herself. "Any words of wisdom from your father?"

"He mostly reminded me to have fun."

"Well. That is one way to look at it."

"I guess." He popped the wrestler in the stomach again. And again. And again.

Soon the door opened for Thorn. Not a minute later, Rocky and Bianca and the redheaded woman swept in.

"Hey, Green Team. Have a seat at the table. As I said, my name is Carol, and I'll be your teacher, your mom, your best friend, your worst enemy, your only contact for this portion of the Gollywhopper Games. You have questions, you ask me. You need to go to the bathroom, you ask me. You need a Band-Aid, you ask me.

"And if you ask me, you're lucky I'm here because

I can be a lot of fun—until you stop following the rules. And that's when I turn into your worst nightmare." Carol raised her auburn eyebrows and flashed a mischievous grin. Then she paced once around the table, smiling and nodding.

"Now, don't ask for hints," she continued. "I won't give them to you. Don't try to bribe me for answers. I wouldn't tell you even if I had them. What I will give you is a guarantee. This day will be one of the most memorable of your lives, win or lose. And I don't like to lose.

"I have this friendly wager with Bill, my counterpart on the red team. You win, and he shaves off every hair from his head. They win, and I shave mine. I like this curly stuff on top of my head. Don't make me lose it. Make me proud.

"How do you start?" Carol leaned on the table for emphasis. "You act like a team. You entered this competition as individuals, but that changes right now. Depend on one another's strengths. Forgive one another's weaknesses. You need that type of attitude. There's a variety of challenges today. And my guess is, any one of you would be hard-pressed to complete them all by yourself. So let's talk about these challenges and the procedures.

"Think of this as a big treasure hunt with one activity leading to the next. You'll have five puzzles you must solve. Each puzzle alternates with a stunt you must perform."

Carol took a seat at the head of the table. "Now, this may sound confusing, but I promise, once you get in there, things'll run as smoothly as a greased pig through buttered hands." Carol referred to the piece of paper in front of her.

"Okay," Carol continued. "Try to follow this. I will lead you to a large warehouse-type area. Inside, you will receive your first puzzle. Each puzzle will have a multiple choice answer—not the same sort of multiple choice you know from school. No. Your choices will be three Golly products. All three will be on a table. The answer to the puzzle is the name of one of those toys or games. Sound easy? It isn't.

"First, you need to solve the puzzle. Be sure your solution makes sense. Be sure you all agree on that solution. Then, and only then, pick up the Golly toy or game that corresponds to the answer. Open it and you'll find an envelope marked STUNT.

"Inside will be instructions on how to perform an activity. Follow the instructions exactly. When you complete the stunt, you'll receive the instructions for the next puzzle. Maybe."

Huh?

"Huh?" said Rocky out loud.

"If you solved the puzzle wrong, it will make you perform the wrong stunt. How will you know you've made a mistake? The puzzle you receive at the end of a wrong stunt will be the very same puzzle you thought you already solved. Then you must go back, figure out the right answer, and perform the right stunt.

"And ouch! That will hurt because you're in a race for time. The team that finishes this treasure hunt with the best time goes on to the next round."

"But," said Rocky, "won't it take more time to sit around and figure out the puzzles than guess and do the stunts?"

"Oh, Rocky, you dear, misguided child. We're smarter than that," said Carol. "Every time you goof, we add a one-minute penalty to your score. So not only have you taken extra time to do more stunts, you also have to deal with those precious extra seconds."

"But—"

"Hold on, Rocky. I'll bet you're still thinking that a one-minute penalty is a small price to pay for a wrong answer, and it'll take longer than that to work the puzzle." Carol shook her head. "According to the rules—and we've worked very hard on them—you must make a true and logical attempt to solve each puzzle. You must work on each for at least five minutes before you make a random guess. We've even installed a five-minute clock visible wherever you are. If you guess wrong, you need to talk it out at least five more minutes before you guess again."

"What if we're smart?" said Bianca. "What if we can figure it out in five seconds? Do we sit around for five minutes anyway?"

"No, no," said Carol. "Each puzzle has a logical answer. And when you find it, you'll know it's right. Our distinguished panel of judges will be able to hear everything you say. If your reasoning is solid and you've legitimately come up with the answer in less than five minutes, move forward as fast as you can. If you try to fool them, they'll know. And they'll stop you.

"Don't try to take any shortcuts. Any infraction of the rules, any failure to follow directions might cost you much more than a minute. It could cost you . . . your hair." Carol's lips crawled to a huge grin. "Just kidding! Your hair's safe. Mine's still at risk."

She paused and studied her paper again. "That's it. Any questions?"

Gil wondered if she could repeat all that, maybe after she'd taken a tranquilizer.

"Of course you have questions. Those directions made no sense to you. But we have to make sure you've heard them. It's the law. Or not. But it is our law." She smiled. "It's not as complicated as it sounds. Really. It's as easy as Puzzle-Stunt, Puzzle-Stunt and so on, five times. The whole process will start flowing once you get in there.

"Oh, and the other team? You'll never see them or hear them. You will, however, hear *about* them. They'll be in a duplicate area, performing the same puzzles and stunts in the exact order. All fair and square. Each time they successfully move to the next puzzle, we'll let you know. And we'll let them know about you.

"If you're wondering about the people who brought you here, they're all safely tucked away upstairs in a sort of stadium luxury box that encircles the entire action area. They'll be able to get up and move around and see and hear everything that happens on both teams. When you get into the room, look up and wave, then forget about them.

"Also forget about the cameras. Dozens of them are camouflaged, but each side will have ten people running around with handheld cameras, capturing everything. We have microphones planted everywhere to pick up every single whisper. At first you may feel self-conscious, but I promise you'll be so focused on the task at hand, they'll soon fade into the sunset."

Carol handed a stapled set of papers to each person. "We do a lot of research at Golly, especially in the Fairview office, where Bill and I work, and we know some people absorb more by listening and some by reading. So everything I've explained is on these sheets. For the next fifteen minutes, all cameras and mikes are off. Take that time to relax and get comfortable with the procedures. Please give one another a chance to read through these. Then you can schmooze all you want. I'll be right back." Carol gave a wink and left, the green door closing behind her.

Gil read through the instructions twice, then looked at the clock on the wall. Carol would be back in about seven minutes.

Bianca was twirling her paper around on the table. Lavinia was still studying. Rocky was sitting on the gorilla, folding his sheets into paper footballs, and Thorn had drifted to the far wall, looking bored.

If Gil was going to do anything about the cheating, it would have to be now. He moved toward Thorn. "We haven't really talked," Gil said, sticking out his hand. "Gil Goodson."

Thorn shook it. "Thorn Dewitt-Formey."

"Is there anything I need to know about you?" asked Gil.

"I don't believe so."

"I'm not trying to be rude, but I mean, is there something about your hearing we should know? Something we could help you with?"

"Oh." Thorn pointed to his ear. "You mean this. Good eyes, Gil."

"Thanks. It's just that I knew a girl," Gil lied, "who was hearing impaired, and it helped if we got her attention first. Should we do anything like that?"

"No. Not necessary. This thing is state of the art. I can hear whispers at thirty feet."

"Really? Battery powered?" Gil craned his neck like he was trying to see it.

Thorn turned his head to oblige. "Smallest battery you'll ever see."

"Really?" Gil amped up the excitement in his voice. "Can you show me?"

By now, Bianca and Rocky had gathered around. Lavinia was staring from the table.

"I don't know," Thorn said. "It's delicate."

"Please," said Gil. "I won't touch it. I only want to see." Slowly, carefully, Gil pulled his lucky penny from his pocket. Too fast and his sweaty hands would drop it. He only had one chance to get this right. He moved the penny from his right hand to his left and plunged that hand into his pocket, the coin pinched between his fingers.

"Yeah, please," said Bianca.

Thorn sighed, dug the piece from his ear, and displayed it in the palm of his hand.

"How long have you been hearing impaired?" Gil asked.

"Most of my life."

"Wow! How do you know what I'm saying right now?" Gil whispered.

"I read lips."

Gil let the penny slip through the hole in his pocket and slide down his leg. It hit the wooden floor with a tiny *clink*.

Thorn's eyes shot to the sound.

"Pennies don't have lips." Gil pointed to the earpiece. "If you stick it back in your ear, I'll make sure the whole world knows. I refuse to be disqualified because they stuck me with cheaters."

Thorn shrugged like he was bored and slipped the earpiece into his shirt pocket.

"And Rocky," Gil said, "the cheating goes for you, too."

"Whoa. I don't have any ear thing."

"I'm not blind, Rocky," said Gil. Then he tugged

his ear and touched his nose like Mr. Titus had. "Neither are the people who run this thing. Your choice: Stop the signals or go home."

"Okay, okay."

Lavinia took an audible breath as if she had been scared to inhale. She lowered her eyes to the table then peeked up at Gil. *Thanks*, she mouthed just before Bianca threw her arms around his neck.

"My hero!" She laughed. "Ooh. Idea here. Every team needs a leader. I elect Gil."

Rocky shook his head. "That'd be a kill. Ask him about his family."

"This isn't about my family, and it isn't about anyone being a leader. We just have to work together if we want to win."

"I want to win," said Bianca.

Gil looked at the others. "Are we gonna win or what?"

"Yeah, we'll win," said Rocky, putting on the game face Gil remembered.

The door swung open. "Sounds like you're ready," said Carol. "Let's play some games."

CHAPTER 11

The five filed behind Carol like first graders following their teacher to recess. If they were a real team, they'd bunch together like every winning team Gil had ever been on. Those teams, though, had practiced for months before their biggest game of the year. Together they learned who was strong and who to avoid in a crunch, who divided the team and who provided the glue.

Watching Rocky swagger in front, Gil was oddly glad he was here. Rocky was the kid you wanted on your team, any team. Kids still talked about that spelling bee in Rocky's fourth-grade class. Five remained on one team; just Rocky and one girl remained on the other, and Rocky's spelling wasn't that impressive. According to the legend, not only did Rocky question his poor teammate over every letter, but his stare rattled the other team so much, every one of them—including Moe, the Human Dictionary—misspelled the same word: *intimidate*.

Bianca could probably handle Rocky's intensity, but Lavinia and Thorn? Lavinia may have been used to scholarship competitions, but Gil doubted she'd seen anyone like Rocky, especially when the fear of losing turned him into a wild man. And Thorn? Big question mark. He seemed so bored, but he must have had his reasons to be here. Why else would he have spent so much money to find an instant winner ticket and also to wire himself up?

Carol led them down another hallway with darkened offices, cordoned-off cubicles, but walls that practically vibrated with color. Where the murals stopped, framed pictures began: formal

portraits of men and women, but with mustaches drawn on them, or with clown hats and squirting bowties, rabbit ears, caterpillar eyebrows, cat's eyes.

The group turned down yet another hall that opened into a junglelike area with flowers and small trees and sunshine that filtered through skylights and floor-to-ceiling windows. They stopped beside a massive pair of green doors in an eight-story brick wall.

Carol turned to them. "Any minute— Correction. Right now, here they are. The other team, with my counterpart, Bill, there in the red shirt."

Bill stopped his team at matching red doors about five yards away, then he and Carol nodded to each other and ruffled their own heads of hair in a silent challenge.

The other team stared at Gil's team, and Gil stared right back until, ghostlike, both sets of doors lumbered open on their own. Gil and his team edged through.

"Oh. My. Gosh," said Bianca.

"Am I hallucinating?" Lavinia asked.

Gil shook his head. "Only if I am."

Palm trees and monstrous flowers rose for stories. Hot-air balloons and skeletons danced from the ceiling. Huge shoes dangled, giant pandas floated around, and gigantic spears of broccoli sprouted from the ground. Puffs of gold confetti rained in random spots, catching the light and casting a brilliance across a small area. A waterfall rushed and rumbled somewhere to his left. And who knew what was beyond that maze of rainbow-colored walls?

"Green team. Green team."

Gil closed his mouth and focused on Carol.

"The wow factor here is huge. It still is for me

after hundreds of times. But now I need you to look up to the spectator area. Wave to everyone." She waited for them to wave. "Now forget they're there. See Jason, the main camera guy to your left? Wave to Jason and his camera. Wave, wave. Good. Now forget him, too.

"But here's something to remember." Carol pointed toward a plain door. "Through there lies a short corridor leading directly to the conference room where we met. We took the long way around and allowed you to make a grand entrance. The conference room can be your second-best friend. Use it as a home base if you find King Kong, the racecar, and all the other random props too distracting. Now come this way."

They stopped at a long, Plexiglas table with green twinkle lights encased along its edges. In the center, on top of a stack of three boxes, sat a green envelope with a big "#1" on it.

"Ta-da! Your first puzzle. When you hear the chimes, open the envelope and begin. I'll be lurking in the shadows if you need me. I'm rooting for you, but by the rules, I'm also your impartial referee and your harshest judge. Do me proud." Carol put on a set of headphones, spoke a few words into the attached microphone, then gave a thumbs-up to someone in the viewing area.

An unbroken line of faces peered from the perimeter of the room. It reminded Gil of feeding time at the zoo. He caught a glimpse of his mom and dad. Then, farther down, Old Man Golliwop. And Mr. Titus, touching his nose and his chin.

Gil stared at Rocky until Rocky noticed.

Rocky looked up at his dad and ran his own finger across his neck. "Satisfied?" he said to Gil.

Blong! Blong! Blong!

Rocky's hand shot out fastest. He grabbed the envelope and ripped it open.

Puzzle #1
* * * * * * * * * * *

Seek A Lively Evil Magician, With Its Terrible Cackling Head
(choose your answer from these three products)

Lavinia spaced out the boxes: The Black Magic Game, The Salem Witch Game, and My First Magic Act.

"I wanna win," said Rocky. "Someone think of something smart to say."

Gil and Lavinia were leaning over the table, staring at the clue. "That's what we're trying to do," said Gil. "Anyone care to help?"

"Or else," Rocky said, lowering his voice, "we can talk real soft, look like we're intelligent and pretend to solve it."

"Why don't we actually solve it?" said Gil.

Bianca and Rocky gathered around. Thorn stood a half step away, looking bored.

Rocky jabbed Gil in the arm. "Look," he said, pointing at Thorn. "The baby's sulking. He misses his ear thing."

"Do not," Thorn said. He moved closer to the group.

Gil tried to ignore the drama and decipher the puzzle. "Seek a lively evil magician, with its terrible cackling head." He turned over the puzzle, looking for directions, clues . . . something.

"Why'd you do that?" said Rocky. "The back's as blank as your mind."

"Shut up and let him think," said Bianca.

Good advice. Gil scanned the warehouse, looking for a grotesque magician with a top hat and magic wand. He saw a tuba, an enormous jar of pickles, but no cackling head. Wait. That wasn't the way to solve it. The answer had to be within the puzzle. He pointed to the paper. "Does anything look strange here?"

"Why does anything have to look strange?" said Rocky. "Well, except for your—Never mind. The puzzle says we're looking for a magician. So that could be The Black Magic Game or My First Magic Act. But it's evil, so that means the first one. But witches can have terrible, cackling heads so it could be The Salem Witch Game."

"In other words," said Bianca, "you have no idea."

Gil shook his head and looked at the clock. They had less than two minutes to figure this out before Rocky would rip open one of those games on his own. Gil felt it.

"Excuse me," said Lavinia, "but I may have the start of an idea."

Maybe Gil had one teammate with a brain.

"The sentence is grammatically incorrect," she said.

"Yeah," said Gil, "I noticed there's no period."

"The sentence also lacks commas."

"There's a comma," said Rocky. "See? 'Seek a lively evil magician—comma—with its terrible cackling head.'"

"But that comma is misplaced. There should be two. One between 'lively' and 'evil' and one between 'terrible' and 'cackling.' Strings of adjectives take commas."

"Maybe," said Gil, "we're supposed to pause where the comma is."

"Perhaps," Lavinia said, "but it's something else, too."

"And that would be . . ." said Rocky.

"The word *its*. A magician is a person, a he or a she. Why would they use 'its' instead of 'his' or 'her'?"

"You may have something," said Gil.

"Ooh," said Bianca. "I might have something else."

"Fleas?" said Rocky.

Bianca shot him a poisonous look. "So I might not be the smartest here—I almost flunked math—but I wrote this history paper about Janice Dickinson, the first supermodel. Don't you love history? Anyway, I would have gotten an *A*, but I capitalized all the letters in the title after my teacher reminded me not to capitalize words like *and* and *with*. And the five stinkin' points she took away brought my paper down to an eighty-nine and—"

"Bianca! You're a genius," said Gil. "You, too, Lavinia. Look. There is a reason for 'its.' Look at the capitalized letters, just the capitalized letters."

As Gil read them, the others chimed in. "S-A-L-E-M-W-I-T-C-H."

Before they reached the "C-H," Rocky had wrestled open the lid of The Salem Witch Game and pulled a card from the green envelope marked STUNT #1.

Stunt #1
* * * * * * * * * *
SEE THE YELLOW STRIPE
ON THE FLOOR?
FOLLOW IT TO THE PIÑATAS.
MORE INSTRUCTIONS
AWAIT YOU THERE.

Rocky raced off. Right as the other four caught up with him, he yanked down an envelope with such force that it shot a wooden pole the size of a large broom handle right toward them. It fell just short and rattled across the floor.

"Rocky!" yelled Bianca. "You could have killed us."

"What? What'd I do?"

Gil rolled his eyes. "Just read it, Rocky."

Rocky held up the message and read it aloud.

Stunt #1
* * * * * * * * * * *

Look above you in the air.
See five piñatas hanging there?
Four contain a gooey brew.
One contains a clue for you.
With all ten hands upon this pole,
strike until you make a hole.
If goo comes out, don't lose all hope—
the next may hold your envelope.

Swaying from near-invisible wires were five piñatas: a black cat, a witch hat, a witch head, a broom, and a cauldron.

"Let's smash the witch in the middle," said Rocky. "Where's the pole?"

"It's what you almost killed us with," Bianca said.

"Here," said Lavinia,who had sneaked away to fetch it.

Rocky grabbed the pole from her hands and reared back to take a swing himself.

"Wait!" Lavinia's scream seemed to startle even herself. "The rule says all ten hands."

"Then get some hands over here," said Rocky.

"I'm at the top," said Thorn, taking the pole away. "Dewitt-Formeys always land on top. It's our family code."

"So tell me," Rocky said. "Is your family code on the family crest on the family flag on the family mansion? What a dweeb!"

"Cut it out, Rocky," said Gil. "Grab the pole."

Rocky latched on underneath Thorn's hands. Then came Lavinia's, Gil's and Bianca's.

With Rocky's power controlling the pole, they reared it back and took a swing. It missed the target, but lifted Thorn off the floor, spilling him away from the group.

"Forget your family code," said Rocky. "We need to organize by height."

Thorn held on at the bottom. Lavinia grasped just above him, then Gil, Bianca, and Rocky. They swiped at the witch. Again. Again. But their pathetic taps only made her sway more.

Gil let go. "Some of us are going left and some are going right, and we're not in sync."

"If we have to do this," said Thorn, "then we need to work it like a crew team so we all swing the same way at the same time."

"Crew team?" said Bianca. "What's a—"

"It's like five people rowing the same boat," said Gil. "When Thorn says, 'stroke,' we all swing this way." Gil nodded his head to his right. "Okay, Thorn. Go!"

"Stroke," said Thorn like the effort to speak would kill him.

They completely missed the witch's head.

"Stroke," he said in a voice that could put a sugar-shocked kid to sleep.

They managed to tap it like the first few tries.

"Stroke," he said with some conviction.

Direct hit.

"Stroke! Stroke!" he yelled.

They were in a rhythm now.

"Stroke! Stroke! Stroke! Stroke!"

"Eew!" A big blob of green goo globbed out and struck Thorn's shoulder. He let go to wipe it off. "Do you know how expensive this shirt is?"

"Have Daddy buy you another one," said Rocky.

Another blob globbed onto Bianca's shoe. She let go. "Gross. It's like—"

"It's not phlegm, Bianca. I promise," said Gil. "You'll be okay."

"C'mon," said Rocky. "We're attacking the cat."

Bianca and Thorn took their places on the pole again.

"Stroke!" Thorn commanded.

A wobbly hit.

"Stroke! Stroke!"

Back in rhythm.

"Stroke! Stroke! Stroke!"

This time a red blob hit Lavinia on the back, but she held on.

"The hat," said Rocky.

"Stroke! Stroke! Stroke! Stroke! Stroke! Stroke!"

A hole—nothing coming out.

"Stroke! Stroke! Stroke!"

The gleam of green paper.

"Stroke! Stroke! Stroke!"

Out fluttered the envelope. Lavinia, quickest to the floor, picked it up.

Before she could open it, Carol made an appearance. Either she materialized from nowhere, or she'd been somewhere in the shadows the whole time.

"You guys," she said. "You did a great job, but if this were the whole ball game, I'd wake up bald tomorrow morning. The other team is ten seconds in front of you. Get moving!"

CHAPTER 12

Lavinia crept her index finger under the flap of the envelope.

"Rip it!" Rocky shouted.

Lavinia jumped, sending the envelope airborne.

Gil snatched it before it landed.

Puzzle #2
* * * * * * * * * * *

"My coat keeps me the warmest during this January freeze," bragged Tracy.
If the above sentence equals ZEBRA,
then what does the following
sentence equal?

The pain in Matthew's elbow lingered
through the month of March.
(Move to table #2,
directly behind the piñatas.)

The only things directly behind the piñatas were one cameraperson, a pair of four-foot dice, and an even larger cup and saucer.

"Who stole table number two?" said Rocky. "Gil?"

Gil spun around, ready to glare. Instead he shot out his arm, alongside Rocky's ear. He pointed. "'Behind,'" Gil said, "depends on where you're standing. Turn around."

Green lights blinked on the other side of the piñatas.

All five ran to the table and gathered around the three boxes: My First Calendar, I Want to Be a Doctor, and Bowling Buddy.

"Oh, great," said Bianca. "I thought I knew this one, but they don't have a math game on the table. There should be a math game."

Gil knew he shouldn't take time to ask. "Why should there be a math game?"

"The sentences are supposed to equal something. Isn't that math?"

"Yeah," said Rocky. "I've never seen math like this."

"Maybe it's not math," said Gil, exhaling.

Rocky exhaled louder. "But they say, 'equal.'"

"The sentences," said Lavinia, "don't need to equal anything mathematically. Logically speaking, if you assign numerical values to the letters according to their positions in the alphabet, the letters in the sentence will add up to more than the letters in the word 'zebra.'"

Rocky snickered. "What'd she say?"

If there was such a thing as a funny nightmare, Gil was in it.

"If it's not math," Bianca said, "what is it?"

"It's boring," said Thorn.

Bianca stuck her tongue out at him. "If you'd help us figure this out, maybe you wouldn't be so bored."

Rocky slapped her on the back. "Good one, Bianca."

Three TV cameras captured that whole scene. Gil wished the cameras could capture the three of them and ship them off to Neptune.

Gil turned his attention to the puzzle, now in Lavinia's hand. "Okay," he said, trying to steer them back. ""My coat keeps me the warmest during this January freeze," bragged Tracy.' What could possibly lead us to the word 'zebra'?"

"I've only been able to rule out things," said Lavinia. "The sentence does not remotely concern a zebra. Zebras don't live in climates with January freezes."

"But last January I went on an African safari, and we saw zebras," said Thorn.

"I don't believe they had you in mind when they designed the puzzle," Lavinia said.

Gil smiled. Go, Lavinia.

They stood in silence, staring at the paper.

"What you said before, Lavinia? That the sentence isn't about zebras? This could be a stretch," Gil said, "but the second sentence mentions March, part of a calendar. So maybe we shouldn't pick My First Calendar. It also talks about elbow pain, so maybe we shouldn't pick I Want to Be a Doctor, either."

Lavinia rubbed her neck. "You're implying that because the sentence doesn't mention bowling, that's the answer, but I can't buy that. The first puzzle literally spelled out the solution."

"Yeah," said Gil. "I thought that was a stretch."

"No, it's a joke," said Rocky. "We're wasting more than penalty minutes looking at this. Let's pick bowling. Now!"

"No," Gil said. "You heard the rules. If we mess up, we need to start—"

"Shush," said Lavinia. "I'm onto something. I was looking for letter patterns. . . ."

"Get to the point," said Rocky.

Lavinia stopped, closed her mouth.

"Forget him," said Bianca. "Keep going."

"Look at this sentence," Lavinia continued. "'"My coat keeps me the warmest during this January freeze," bragged Tracy.' It contains all the letters in the word 'zebra'."

Gil blinked. The letters popped at him, right there—all the letters together. "Look. Between 'freeze' and 'bragged'. Slide the two words together and—"

"Find the word in the second sentence already," said Rocky.

Gil and Bianca read together, "The pain in Matthew's elbow lingered through—"

"Bowling," said Bianca.

Rocky grabbed the box. "That's what I was going to open ten hours ago."

"Cool!" said Bianca. "'Elbow' and 'lingered' together. I mean, how did someone think that up? Those Golly people must be really smart. You, too, Lavinia, for figuring it out."

"Of course, you were the one to first notice *bowling*."

"I was, wasn't I?"

"That's so sweet," said Rocky, mimicking their voices and mangling the Bowling Buddy box to get at the envelope. "But now," he said, his normal tone returning, "stop gabbing like a bunch of old ladies, and come look at this stunt."

Stunt #2
* * * * * * * * * * *

IT'S ONE, TWO . . .
FIVE STRIKES, YOU'RE IN.
JUST FIND THE GIANT,
WHITE BOWLING PIN.

They raced toward the rear of the room where a bowling pin, at least ten feet tall, swayed from the ceiling over a regulation bowling lane. Instructions dangled.

Stunt #2
* * * * * * * * * * *

LET'S GO BOWLING!

YOUR GOAL:
You must knock down all the pins five times.

AS IN REGULATION BOWLING:
You must stand behind the red foul line
when you roll the ball.

UNLIKE REGULATION BOWLING:
You may roll as many balls
as it takes to knock all the pins over.

AS IN REGULATION BOWLING:
The pins will reset automatically.

UNLIKE REGULATION BOWLING:
Your best bowler can do most of the bowling.
<u>But each of you must knock down</u>
<u>at least five pins.</u>

"I bowl," said Gil, shoving the rules into his pocket. "Who else bowls?"

"I do," said Rocky.

"I bowled once at a birthday party in first grade," Lavinia said. "It wasn't that difficult."

"Good," said Thorn, sitting down. "This is the first bowling thing I've seen."

"I've been bowling, but I'm terrible," said Bianca. "Can I go first to get it over with?"

"Go," Gil said. "It'll be easier to knock down your five when all ten are standing. Then Rocky or I will take over after that."

Bianca walked to the foul line with one of the five green balls and stuck her fingers into its holes. She swung the ball back and forth. Back and forth. Back and forth. Then she released it. The ball sailed in the air and landed six feet down the lane with a thunk. "Oh, no!"

"What's wrong, Bianca?" asked Gil. "Your ball's going straight. Watch! Watch! Seven!"

"It's not that. I broke a nail."

"Big deal," said Rocky, already posing, ball in hand. He took the classic four-step approach and thundered the ball down the lane, toppling two more pins. Not waiting for his ball to return, he picked up another and rolled it, wiping out the last pin.

"Great, Rocky!" Gil patted him on the back, then plopped a ball into Thorn's lap.

Thorn turned it around a few times. "Which fingers go where?"

"No time for a lesson," said Rocky. "Just get up and go."

Thorn heaved the ball at the pins. It bounced twice and skipped into the gutter. He tried another. Gutter. Another. Gutter again.

"I've got a really, really good idea," said Bianca. "Do it the kid way."

"Excuse me?" said Thorn.

Rocky grabbed the ball from Thorn and thudded it behind the foul line. "Now straddle the ball, and shove it from behind."

Thorn did, and the ball wobbled, creeping down the lane, trying to decide to go straight or veer left.

Before it got to the pins, Rocky thunked down a second ball. "Don't wait. Go again."

Thorn shoved
it, too.

All five of them
stood there for what
seemed an eternity, wait-
ing for the balls to strike.

"Hey, Rocky," said Gil. "Something look strange
to you?"

"Yeah. I've never seen a ball move that slowly."

Gil shook his head. "I mean, down the lane. See?"

"I see he knocked down three pins. And that second one is gonna hit more."

"Yay, Thorn!" Bianca said. "Six. You're done."

"My turn again." Rocky grabbed the ball and
rolled. By the time he hit three more, he had another ball in his hands.

"Wait," said Gil. "Something looks strange."

"Your face."

Gil ignored him. "There's tons of markings on the lane."

"They always have those arrows so you know where to aim."

"Rocky," said Gil. "Look again. This one has too many, and they're circles, not arrows."

"Let me see." Rocky put down the ball and started running up.

"Stop!" Lavinia said. "You can't go over the foul line."

"The rules say don't bowl over the foul line. You don't see me bowling,

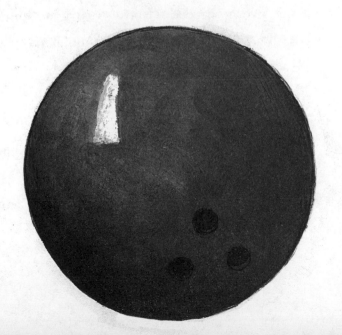

do you?" Rocky skidded to a stop. "Hey! Some of these circles have lit-up letters. I've never seen anything like it." He bent to inspect.

"Come back, Rocky!" shouted Gil. "I bet we get a letter for every pin we knock down."

Rocky ran and skidded back. The second he stepped onto the right side of the foul line, Gil bowled one ball, then another. Thorn's last pin, down.

"What letter did you get?" shouted Rocky.

"Forget the letters until we knock down all the pins. Go, Lavinia."

She rolled the ball down the lane as if she had been doing it for years. Six pins fell.

When Gil finished off the other four—giving him the five he needed—Rocky was right behind him with a ball. He launched it as soon as the pins had reset. A strike.

"You're on a roll, Rocky. Finish up," said Gil, feeding him another ball.

Rocky rolled two balls in rapid-fire succession, wiping out all ten.

The team raced to the little circles on the lane. Each contained a lit-up letter.

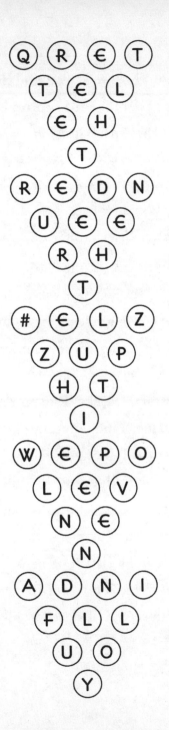

"Perfect," said Rocky. "If you read Swahili."

"I've been there," said Thorn. "Or rather, Kenya, where they speak it. That's where I saw the zebras."

"La-di-flaming-da," said Rocky. "Someone translate this."

"I can't see all the letters at once," said Bianca. "How do you expect me to read it?"

"Who has a pencil?" Gil asked, digging in his pocket for the bowling rules.

"We left everything in the conference room," said Thorn. "Everything." He glared at Gil.

Ancient history. "Rocky. Run to the conference room," Gil said. "Find anything to write with. That way, past the flamingos. Hurry."

Rocky zoomed, dodging a full-sized pink Cadillac, disappearing behind a counter from an old-time diner, returning faster than possible with a pad of paper and a fistful of pens.

"I'll yell out the letters," said Bianca.

After she finished, Gil stared at his paper.

QRETTELEHTREDNUEE
RHT# ELZZUPHTIWEPO
LEVNEN ADNIFLL UOY

"This has to make sense," Gil said.

"Could it be an anagram?" asked Lavinia.

"No," said Gil. "They wouldn't make us rearrange fifty different letters. Besides, one's a pound sign."

"Cryptogram?" she said. "Where letters of the alphabet stand for different ones?"

"No way," said Rocky. "Carol said one puzzle, one stunt. We did our puzzle. We did our stunt. We want our next puzzle. Hey, Carol! Where's puzzle number . . . What puzzle's next?"

"Number three," said Thorn. "Only number three."

"Hey, Carol lady! You need—"

"Forget it, Rocky." Gil smiled. "I got it."

"Can you share it with the class?"

Gil didn't waste his time with a dirty look. "We wrote down the letters backward. We should've started at the bottom with the letter closest to us."

Lavinia read, "You'll find an envelope with puzzle number three under the letter *Q*."

They raced up the lane.

"How do you get underneath a letter?" said Rocky.

Lavinia knelt by the *Q*. "Ah. It's a pull tab like cans have." She pawed at it.

Bianca scooted Lavinia's hand over. "You'll have to thank me double if I sacrifice another fingernail." She popped up the *Q*, and along with it came an inch-thick plug of wood the size of a silver dollar.

Inside was a tiny green envelope.

CHAPTER 13

Rocky lunged for the envelope in Bianca's hands.

She whirled around. "I got it out. It's mine to open." Bianca cleared her voice, pulled out the paper, and held it up. "It's a poem thing and some numbers. Here." She gave the paper to Gil.

Puzzle #3

* * * * * * * * * * *

Winds batter palm trees,
scatter splinters everywhere.
The island renews.
20, 9, 17, 26, 1, 3
(Your choices are on table #3, in back of the
bowling pin setter.)

They bolted to the back of the bowling lane and almost banged into Carol and a cameraperson. "You're making me one happy camper," Carol said. "You gained a few seconds." Like a bat, she disappeared into the shadows.

"I wish she'd stop wasting our time," said Rocky.

"I heard that!" Carol's voice echoed from somewhere.

"You're the one wasting our time, Rocky," said Bianca.

Gil tried to ignore the quibbling. "Here are our choices: Hurricane Island, Strewn, or I'm a Poet! (Don't I Know It!). "

Rocky slapped the table. "These puzzles have no directions. They make no sense," he said. "I'm gonna sit here and watch the clock. After five minutes, I'm opening something."

"You can't make that decision for us," said Bianca.

"You heard the lady. We did good last time. I bowled great, I ran fast, and we gained what? Like ten seconds? We'll do it my way unless you solve it in"—he looked at the clock—"four minutes and twelve seconds, nine, eight . . ."

"Please stop," said Lavinia. "I can't think when you're counting."

"Then let me think for you," said Rocky. "If that poem had a name, it would be called Hurricane. So that's my choice in three minutes and fifty-one seconds."

Bianca glared at him. "Listen to what you said. 'If that *poem* had a name—' Poem. Why shouldn't the answer be I'm a Poet?"

"Looking at it another way, the poem speaks of splinters scattering everywhere," said Lavinia. "That brings to mind the word *strewn*."

"What about the numbers?" Gil said. "We can't leave those out."

"He's right. The numbers." Lavinia looked down at the puzzle. "The highest number is twenty-six, so the numbers could correspond to letters of the alphabet."

Gil did some quick figuring. "They could if T-I-Q-Z-A-C spelled a word."

"Six letters," said Lavinia. "Strewn has six letters."

Thorn pointed to the box. "I was thinking Strewn myself."

"He speaks," said Bianca.

"Why, Thorn?" asked Gil.

"Totally different reason. I've never seen Strewn, and I have every Golly video game. This would be the perfect opportunity for Golly to start advertising a new product. When my father's company launches a new product, they—"

"I don't know," said Gil, cutting him off, watching Rocky watch the clock. "You might be right, but we need to solve the puzzle."

"It may help," said Lavinia, "if we're all quiet for a moment."

Rocky pointed to the clock. "You got two minutes and forty moments."

Gil looked at the clock, looked at the puzzle. Clock. Puzzle. Clock. Puzzle. Cameraperson. Clock. Puzzle. Then at Lavinia, leaning against an eight-foot rubber duckie, her hand shielding her eyes. Maybe she would come up with something again—at least something that would get one of them to think in the right direction.

"I can't stand the silence," said Bianca. "Maybe we should do it Rocky's way."

"We still have almost a minute and a half," said Gil.

Lavinia tapped him on the shoulder. "Do you think it matters that the poem is a haiku?"

"High what?" said Rocky.

"Haiku. Japanese poetry form. Three lines, five syllables in the first and third lines and seven in the second."

"Doubtful," said Gil. "That adds up to seventeen, and the numbers go up to twenty-six. Any other ideas?"

"Ooh," Bianca said. "Maybe this is a bad idea. But the first puzzle's answer was in the second box. And the second puzzle's was in the third box. So maybe this one's in the first box."

"Three, two, one . . . First box it is." Rocky ripped open Hurricane Island.

"Rocky!" Bianca's face matched her nail polish. "We didn't all agree. If it's wrong, we're suing you for a million dollars apiece. What fun is it if you decide?"

"Too late now."

Gil wanted to smack the smug look off Rocky's face, but Rocky had one thing right: It was too late.

"Says here we go to the trees."

They sprinted left to the palm trees poking into the warehouse sky.

Rocky had the envelope opened before Thorn brought up the rear.

Stunt #3
* * * * * * * * * * *

**Five different climbers
must each fetch a coconut
from one of five palm trees.
When you have all five, open them.
You'll find what you need for your next puzzle.**

"I've never climbed a tree," said Bianca.

"They're not really trees," Gil said. "See? They're utility poles with hooks jutting out. It's as easy as climbing a ladder."

"I've never climbed a ladder," said Thorn.

"Me either," said Bianca, "but I'm going up anyway."

Gil left the drama, scrambled up his tree, grabbed his coconut, and scampered down.

Lavinia was a step behind Gil. She could climb. She could bowl. She could think. "That was great," she said, catching up to Gil. "I've been wanting to go to a climbing wall, but Mother's leery about heights.

At least this was close." She let loose a huge smile.

It was infectious. "You were quick, Lavinia," Gil said. "And I don't mean this in a bad way, but you don't seem athletic."

"I do other things besides academic events. I'm the center on my school's field hockey team. Colleges like multifaceted applicants."

Gil pictured her weaving down the field in shin guards and a plaid skirt. She'd almost be—

"Gil!" Rocky was purple, and he was standing with Thorn at the base of Thorn's tree.

"What?"

Rocky pointed. "This yellow-bellied butthead won't climb."

Gil looked up. Thorn's coconut was still at the top. "You didn't go up?"

"I don't do heights," Thorn said, his permanently red cheeks growing redder.

"C'mon," said Bianca, clutching her coconut. "I thought Dewitt-Formeys always land on top. Here's your chance."

"That's not—"

"Here's the deal, Thorn," said Gil. "If you don't do

this, we stand here like total idiots until the other team wins. You want the world to see that on TV?"

Thorn stood stone still, his lips now a funny shade of gray.

Rocky picked up Thorn and threw him over his shoulder. "Admit I'm strong."

"Oh, no," said Thorn. "You're not carrying me up."

Rocky put him down. "I just wanted you to see you can trust me. I'll hold on to you," he said, putting on the team face Gil remembered. "Can you take two steps up?"

Thorn did.

Rocky latched onto his calf. "I'm right behind you. Take one more step. I will, too. I'll hold on to you the whole time. Ten steps, grab your coconut, and drop it so you have both hands free to climb down."

Just then, Carol didn't show up, but her voice did. "The red team is about to start puzzle number four. No penalty seconds."

Thorn took a third step. Then a fourth. "How many more?"

"You're almost halfway," called Gil.

Thorn glanced toward him.

"Don't look down," said Gil. "Look to your goal."

Thorn and Rocky chugged up and, within a minute, Thorn dropped his coconut at Bianca's feet, breaking it open.

The trip down took even less time, and when Thorn put his second foot on the ground, he gave his first real smile and shook Rocky's hand. "I did it. I actually did it."

Gil patted Thorn on the back, then spun around.

Rocky had already climbed back up one of the poles with two coconuts. He dropped them down, and they broke. Gil slammed the other two to the ground with the same results.

"I have envelope number one," said Gil, pulling out the paper. "Says, 'Winds batter palm trees.'"

Lavinia continued, "'Scatter splinters everywhere.'"

"Oh no," said Bianca. "It's puzzle number three again. Rocky!"

Gil's stomach dropped faster than coconuts to the ground. "Back to table three. And we need to get serious."

"I've been thinking about the puzzle the whole time," Lavinia said as she ran alongside Gil. "It's in the numbers and how they relate to the poem."

"Keep going."

"If the first number, 20, is the twentieth letter of the poem . . ."

"I hope you're right," said Gil.

Gil grabbed the puzzle when they reached the table.

Winds batter palm trees,

scatter splinters everywhere.

The island renews.

20, 9, 17, 26, 1, 3

"I think Lavinia figured it out," Gil said. "Give us a second. You count the twentieth letter in the poem, Lavinia. I'll count the ninth."

"Twentieth is *S*."

"Ninth is *T*, and it's obvious the last two are *W* and *N*. Open Strewn, Rocky."

Stunt #3

✳ ✳ ✳ ✳ ✳ ✳ ✳ ✳ ✳ ✳ ✳

Welcome to the world of Strewn, Golly's newest video game. Not only did Captain Savage's disabled ship wash onto the sands of a deserted island, but the ship exploded, scattering bits and pieces of important items around that island. As he and his surviving crew of four investigate, they find this isn't the first time survivors have been stranded here. The island is strewn with other potentially lifesaving objects. You've found a stockpile of useful tools, but unfortunately a beast guards them. It's your mission to search the island for the five swords you need to slay the beast. Find the island, find the swords, slay the beast. Go.

"Anybody see an island?" asked Bianca.

"Not since Fiji," said Thorn.

Gil climbed onto the table, couldn't see much but . . . "I heard water earlier. Hear that?"

Bianca pointed. "It's coming from this direction."

Gil leaped from the table and started running. Past an orange pickup truck, over a sleeping hippopotamus, around a ten-foot blue zucchini, through the mouth and out the tail of a whale.

And there it was. Tiny waves rippled from the floor and spilled onto sand. The shoreline edged a

jungle with a waterfall and caves and live trees and real flowers.

They jumped over the three feet of ocean, onto the beach, and into the jungle.

"Everyone spread out," said Gil. "Look for swords. Find the beast."

Gil swiped his way through enormous leaves, working toward the deepest point of the island, examining flower stems, running his hands up and down tree trunks, climbing over boulders. Over boulders? What about under?

Gil put his shoulder to one, tried to move it. It budged. Tried another. Stuck solid. Back to the first. Push. Push. Again. It tipped half an inch. "Rocky! Over here. I need more muscle."

Rocky ran through the jungle brandishing a blade. "I found this against a tree. Whaddaya need?"

"Help me shove the rock."

With double the strength, the boulder tilted over. Sword underneath. "That's two."

"Three," said Rocky. "Your girlfriend, Lavinia, has one. Don't know about Bianca, but I think Thorn's lounging on the beach waiting for the butler to bring him his caviar."

"Leave him alone, Rocky. He's harmless."

"And useless."

Gil couldn't disagree. "Two swords over here," he yelled. "Anyone else?"

"I have one," said Lavinia.

"Me too," called Bianca.

Nothing from Thorn.

"Were any buried in the sand?" yelled Gil. No reply. "Then everyone to the beach."

Lavinia had found her sword on top of a cave and Bianca's was in the ground next to a group of flowers. Thorn had already sifted through one quarter of the sand.

They spread over the expanse of beach, Rocky kicking through the sand, Lavinia on her hands and knees, Bianca shuffling back and forth, and Gil and Thorn leaning over and running their fingers through the five-foot-wide strip.

Where was it? Where was it?

"By the way," said Thorn, "I did find the beast. It's in that cave."

Where was that fifth sword, though? Maybe three of them should continue looking in the jungle, but Gil felt sure the fifth one was here. If no one found it in—

"Yo!" said Rocky. "Found it."

Back into the jungle, into the cave. An enormous silver creature with glowing red eyes growled at them. Rocky rammed a sword into a hole in its side. "Kill the sucker!"

"Oh, gross!"

"No blood, Bianca," said Gil. "It's not alive."

"Hand me another," said Rocky. He shoved the other four into the preformed holes, one by one. After the fifth, the beast groaned then keeled over with a vibrating thud.

Gil dropped to the ground on all fours to where the beast had been standing. Thankfully the writing there had nothing to do with winds battering palm trees.

Carol reappeared from nowhere. "Major mistake, major. But you're still in this. Just stop driving me nuts. Even if I don't have to shave my hair, I'll have to color it instead. It's turning gray before my eyes. Now make up that four and a half minutes!"

"Less than five minutes?" said Gil. "We can do this." He read the puzzle written on the ground, then he read it again more slowly, at Bianca's request.

Puzzle #4

* * * * * * * * * * *

Call 1-33-784-693-6557.

(Follow the blue line to table #4.)

The blue line zigged and zagged, sending the green team around the giant dice again, circling a golden grand piano, passing a people-sized ant farm, and stopping at a living room with sofas, tables, overstuffed chairs, and their three choices: Wonder Tiny Dolls, Busy Busy Babies, or Destiny Dolls.

"There's the phone," said Bianca, pointing to the table next to the sofa. "Let's call."

Rocky grabbed the receiver. "Who remembers the number?"

"I don't remember it," said Bianca, "but I wrote it on my hand when Gil said it again."

"So shoot."

"Put it on speaker phone," said Thorn, "so we all hear."

"How—"

"That's one thing I know." Thorn hung up, pushed a button that broadcast the dial tone, then punched in the numbers from Bianca's hand.

"That's more numbers than a normal long-distance call," said Lavinia.

"This isn't exactly a normal place," Gil said.

The phone rang and rang and rang.

"C'mon," said Rocky, "pick up, you incompe-
tents." He stared at the phone. "What if he dialed
wrong? I'm hanging up." He looked around. "If no
one objects."

"Go ahead," said Bianca.

Rocky pushed the speaker phone button, then
redialed.

Beep. Beep. Beep.

"Busy?" said Gil. "As in Busy Busy Babies?"

Rocky's hand reached for the box, but Bianca
shoved it away. "No," she said. "It wasn't busy the
first time."

"She's right about that," said Gil. "But, Bianca,
are you sure the number's right?"

"With her, anything's possible. I'll go and . . ."
Rocky sprinted off mid-sentence.

"This is not going as well as I anticipated,"
Lavinia said.

Gil nodded. "The other team could still mess up.
We just need to play our own game."

"And don't let anyone bully us into the wrong
answers," Thorn said.

Bianca sighed. "I got that number right, I'm sure."

"It was a long number, Bianca," said Gil.

"They could have made it easier, like when I order my Moonglo makeup. You know, Lavinia, when you decide to wear make-up, you need to get Moonglo mascara. It doesn't make you look like a raccoon if you get something in your eye—like an eyelash or a tear. But what I mean is, you know how companies make it easy to remember phone numbers? Like I dial one eight hundred Moonglo, and I don't have to remember numbers or anything. Which is good because—"

"We know," said Gil. "You're not good at math."

"Yeah," said Bianca, "but my point is if one thirty-three-something-something-something spelled a word—"

Gil grabbed her shoulders. "Bianca, you're a genius."

"I am?"

"Sometimes you are. Now repeat the numbers."

Before she could, Rocky showed up. "I'm back. First number is one."

"Aah!" said Gil. "The number one on the phone doesn't have any letters."

"Maybe," Bianca said, "they wanted to trick us into believing it was a phone number."

"Maybe so." Gil moved to the phone. "Next number."

"Three," said Rocky.

"When I text, that's D, E, or F," Bianca said.

"Okay," Gil said. "Do any of the dolls start with any of those letters?"

Lavinia grabbed a box. "Destiny Dolls. Maybe the numbers spell out Destiny Dolls."

"Huh?" Rocky's eyebrows came together. "Are you idiots? Numbers don't spell."

Thorn explained what they were doing as Bianca, Lavinia, and Gil worked their system.

"We already have *D*," said Lavinia, reading the label on the Destiny Dolls box. "Next, *E*."

"Three again," responded Bianca.

"Right again," confirmed Gil.

"S."

"Seven."

"Keep going."

T-I-N-Y. Check. Check. Check. Check. D-O-L-L-S.

Gil pumped his fist. "Yes!"

"My turn again," said Rocky. "I get to open that Destiny Do-Goody. Gimme." He snatched the box from Bianca.

"*Stop!*"

With Lavinia's booming command, Rocky jumped, dropped the box.

Lavinia grabbed Gil's hand. "The clue says, 'Call one thirty-three,' and so on. We've completely discounted the number one. So far, everything in the clues has had a purpose."

"What are you thinking?" asked Gil.

Rocky tapped his foot.

"Shut up!" Bianca scowled at him.

Lavinia took a deep breath. "We need to examine our choices again. Destiny Dolls might be right."

"Busy Busy Babies can't be right because the phone rang the first time," said Bianca.

"That leaves Wonder Tiny dolls," said Gil. "Won-der-Ti-ny-Dolls," he repeated slowly, stressing each syllable. "And if the 'one' of the phone number is spelled . . ."

"*W-O-N*," Lavinia continued, picking up Gil's train of thought, "then the remaining letters and numbers might match up. Let's try it."

"Okay, Lavinia, give me the first letter after *W-O-N*?"

"Next is *D*," she said, running the drill again.

"Three on the phone," said Bianca.

"Right," confirmed Gil.

"Then *E*."

"Three."

"Yeah."

As they ran through the letters, Rocky inched toward the other box. Bianca held onto it with a death grip until the last letter checked out. "It's yours, Rocky."

He ripped at it, dislocating the doll's head, then slashed open the envelope.

Stunt #4
* * * * * * * * * * *

Wonder Tiny Dolls are small,
but one has grown up very tall.
And now she's not a pretty sight.
Please help—she's over to your right.

Rocky raced off, leading the others to a huge chair with an enormous doll body—at least five times the size of an adult—seated four feet off the ground and minus head, arms, and legs.

"Eew!" said Bianca.

"That's certainly gruesome," said Lavinia.

"Too bad there's no blood," said Rocky. "You'd think with this amount of dismembering going on, there'd be gallons of it smeared all over her little pink dress."

"It's a pinafore," said Bianca.

"And you're a pinhead."

Thorn stayed out of the Ping-Pong match and opened a second envelope marked for that stunt.

Stunt #4
* * * * * * * * * * * *

The crew at the factory didn't have time to put me
together yesterday.
If you attach all my body parts correctly, I'll give
you your next puzzle.

"And here are the parts," said Gil.

A jumble of toes, feet, shins, and thighs; fingers, hands, forearms, and upper arms; ears, eyes, nose, lips, hair, and one huge head were heaped in a green tub to the side of the doll body.

"Leave the giant head in the tub," Gil said. "We need to separate the other pieces into face parts, arm parts, and leg parts."

Gil picked up a nose, an eyeball, and a plug of hair. He looked up to where the head would go. Too high to reach. "You guys finish. I'm going to find something to climb on." He took only a couple steps. "Rocky, come here and grab one of these ladders. Set it up on that side. Thorn, you don't climb, so you'll put the toes into the feet. Lavinia, do the fingers."

"I get the face," said Bianca.

"Perfect." Gil set up his ladder. Ran to get an upper arm. Needed to make up some time. He grabbed the arm and—

It flew into the air, but he caught it. He needed to slow down. Wipe his palms. Hold the arm. Climb the ladder. No. Too dangerous. "Bianca, do me a favor. Hand me this arm after I've climbed high enough. Give Rocky his, too."

Gil tried to insert the arm's six-inch screw into the shoulder socket, but he couldn't get the right angle. He climbed a step higher, then a step lower. No and no. It looked like Rocky was having the same problem.

Gil climbed down, dropped the doll's arm, and scooted his ladder to Rocky's side. He supported the end of that upper arm while Rocky eased it into place. Gil rotated the arm clockwise as far up as he could reach.

Rocky took a step higher, grabbed the stump, and sent it down to Gil. After about five rotations, the arm set snug in the shoulder.

With the ladders still set there, they went to work on the lower left arm.

Bianca acted as their parts runner. Even so, she worked fast enough to also pop the eyes into their sockets, wedge the nose into the middle of the face, screw in the ears, attach the lips, jam in sixteen hair plugs, and tell them of each accomplishment by the time the arms were in place.

"How're you guys coming?" Gil called to Lavinia and Thorn.

"Two more fingers," Lavinia said.

"Three more toes."

"Two more hair plugs," said Bianca.

"Ready for the head, Rocky?"

Rocky grunted and grabbed his ladder and

positioned it left of the neck while Gil put his to the right. He took two steps up.

"Done," Bianca said.

"Okay, now hand me the head."

Bianca bent over, grabbed the doll by the ear, and managed to lift the head a couple feet off the ground. "It's heavy."

"It can't be that heavy," said Rocky.

"It is."

Gil leaped down and lifted the head. "She's not joking, Rocky. This sucker is really heavy. No way we can hold it and climb a ladder. Lavinia, Thorn, Bianca," he said. "See if the three of you can hand the head to us."

Those three stood behind the doll's chair and raised the giant head above their own. From their ladder perches, neck high, Gil and Rocky reached for the head, but the ear holds were still half a foot too low.

Rocky grabbed at the hair, but a plug came out with his first swipe.

"Now look what you've done," Bianca said. "I'll fix it."

"I have an idea," said Gil. He climbed another couple rungs and surveyed the contents of the warehouse. He saw the palm trees and the giant bowling pin, the tip of the golden piano and living room. The living room. There was something he had seen on the way from the living room. Something. Something. There! He clambered down the ladder and tugged Rocky out of Bianca's face. "Come on."

Without question, Rocky ran alongside Gil. Together they hauled back one of that giant pair of dice and shoved it against the doll's chair. They hoisted the head on top of that, but it left room for only one person to stand with it.

"Lavinia, jump up there, okay?"

Lavinia hopped up a few rungs of the ladder and jumped onto the four-foot die. She lifted the head high enough for Gil and Rocky to take it from her and set the giant screw into the socket in the doll's neck. Gil twisted the chin to Rocky. Rocky sent it back to Gil. They spun the chin round and round until the head was fully on and facing front.

By this time, Bianca and Thorn had attached the hands and the leg parts. They were each twisting a foot into place.

"That's it," Thorn said. "We did it!"

Nothing.

"Where's our envelope?" said Rocky.

"We must have done something wrong," said Lavinia.

Rocky and Gil rechecked the arms and head. The others examined the reachable parts. Everything seemed tight. Now what? They stood back and stared.

"Is it me," said Bianca, "or do the doll's feet look funny?"

"Two left feet," said Gil.

"Hey, Carol!" Bianca said. "Wherever you are! They gave us two left feet."

"No, Bianca," said Gil. "We gave her two left feet. We just need to move some toes. The big toe goes on the inside."

Gil and Rocky jumped to it, switching around four of the toes on the right foot—the middle toe, already correct. One last twist to the baby toe and *pow!* The doll lit up. And from her pinafore popped an envelope. Success!

But had they made up any time?

CHAPTER 15

"**G**ood news and bad news," said Carol, ruffling her hair. "There's hope for me yet. The red team messed up that last puzzle. They made the mistake you almost did: forgot to use the one in the phone number. But the bad news is you're still nine seconds behind."

Gil didn't wait until Carol disappeared. He looked at the next puzzle. "Huh?"

"Share." Bianca pulled the paper away and glanced at it. "Her what?" With a twist of her wrist, she flicked the paper outward for someone else to take.

Puzzle #5

* * * * * * * * * * *

**Her hound do whirl done bag hag gun.
(Table #5 is on the wall at the opposite
side of the room.)**

The team hurried across the area, passing the puzzle back and forth, sighing.

Gil felt the puzzle return to his hands. He read it again. *Her hound do whirl done bag hag gun.* "Could they make this one any stranger?" Maybe their choices would give him some clue: Around the World and Back Again, The Great Crook Chase, or Word Scurry.

"Sounds like a scurry of words to me," said Bianca.

"I wish I knew how to figure things out like the rest of you," Thorn said. "I wish I knew what it meant."

"Well, it does mean something," said Lavinia.

"I want to say it means nothing," said Rocky.

"You always say that," Bianca said, "and you've been right how many times?"

"Okay," said Gil. "What if we each copy the puzzle then work alone for three minutes?"

No one disagreed.

Gil took his copy and sat next to five stairs leading nowhere. He stared at the words. *Her hound do whirl done bag hag gun.* He could rearrange the letters. Or divide them in different places. Those ideas didn't work.

He could group the first letters of each word, then the second letters and so on: *hhdwdbhg eoohoaau ruinggn nre dl.* Nope. Skip every other letter? *hrondwiloeahgu ehudohrdnbgagn.* Or not. Write it backward? *nuggahgabenodlrihwoddnuohreh.* No again.

Beep. Beep. Beep. Thorn's watch sounded the end of their silent time.

Gil returned to the other four. "Anyone?"

They responded with head shakes and shoulder shrugs.

"Maybe we start opening," said Rocky. "Maybe we'll get lucky."

"Maybe not," said Bianca. "But this silent thing didn't work for me, either."

"Then talk," said Gil. "What do you think when you look at the puzzle, Bianca?"

"Just that this sounds like one of those higgledy-piggledy nursery rhymes that never made any sense, either. You know, like a scurry of words."

"Sounds like someone's bagging a hag with a gun—cops and crooks to me," said Rocky.

"Oh, no," Gil said. "We're not doing that again. Until we know we're right, we're not opening another thing. Lavinia? You have any thoughts?"

"Not yet."

"Thorn?"

"I'm bad at this," he said, "but I keep thinking it's that Around the World game—"

"I know, because you've been there, and it sounds like some foreign language you heard in Outer East Mongolia."

"Rocky!" yelled Bianca. "Shut it."

"Actually," said Thorn, "he's not too far off. I was going to say Sweden, though."

"This puzzle's in Swedish?" asked Bianca. "I

don't know Swedish. Do you know Swedish, Thorn?"

"A few words. I had a Swedish nanny. She spoke English, but with a Swedish accent. And if you say this sort of fast, it sounds like you're mimicking her. Try it."

Gil shrugged. Anything was worth a try. "Her hound do whirl done bag hag gun."

"No," said Thorn. "Sort of run the words together and make your voice go higher and lower like this." Thorn repeated the words in a lilting manner, accenting every other syllable. "HerHOUNDdoWHIRLdoneBAGhagGUN."

"Do it again," said Gil.

Thorn did.

"Keep going."

As Thorn repeated it smoother and faster, again and again, Gil glanced at their choices.

"Bingo!" he said. "Thorn's right: Around the World and Back Again."

"You're just saying that," said Rocky.

"It is right," said Gil. "Don't you hear it?"

Bianca shook her head.

"Sorry, Gil," said Lavinia. "I don't hear it, either."

"Read it out loud, then, Lavinia."

"Her hound do whirl done bag hag gun." She stated each word as its own island.

Gil wanted to scream. He could hear it so clearly. He took a deep breath. "Okay. Slur the first two words together. 'Her hound' becomes 'heround,' which is 'around.' 'Do' is 'the'—"

"'Whirldone' is 'world and' back again. Got it," said Lavinia.

"Me too!" said Bianca.

Thorn didn't wait to hear from Rocky. He had the box opened and the envelope out.

"Hey, Carol," yelled Rocky. "The other team this far yet?"

Her voice came from some surround-sound speaker. "Can't tell you till it's over."

At least it wasn't over.

"Hurry," said Rocky.

Thorn held up the paper.

Stunt #5

* * * * * * * * * * *

If you still want to win,
then take off and fly
toward the hot-air balloons
floating high in our sky.

They raced in the same direction, to seven hot-air
balloons suspended in midair. One had descended
enough so that Rocky could jump and grab a second
envelope dangling from the basket.

Stunt #5

* * * * * * * * * * *

You first need to push the button.
It's green, in the shape of a star.
Then race and collect the five toys or games
that let you get this far.

Beep-beep! Beep-beep!

The sound sprang from the ground, causing all five
of them to back away. A column rose from the floor.
When it stopped, a green star lit the top. Rocky
pushed it, and it started blinking.

"Okay," said Gil, looking all around. "Where was everything?"

"That's easy," said Bianca. "This is like a giant shopping mall without the clothes." She pointed to her left. "The Around the World game is just over there. The Wonder Tiny Doll's in the living room that way. That Strewn game is behind the bowling alley. The bowling game is near the piñatas . . . and what was the first?"

"Salem Witch," said Lavinia.

"At the front door."

"Rocky, you get that one," said Gil. "Thorn, get Around the World."

"I remember where Strewn is," said Lavinia.

"Go," said Gil. "Bianca, get the doll, and I'll get bowling."

Gil raced toward the direction Bianca had pointed, and within seconds, saw two of the piñatas still swaying from a distance. He made his legs go as fast as he'd ever felt them move. He propelled around one object then another, not noticing colors or details; just shapes to avoid. He found the table, still with its blinking lights, and picked up the pieces of the Bowling Buddy box that Rocky had mangled.

Gil swung around, retracing his steps, and spotted only the polka-dotted balloon to help lead him back.

When he returned, Thorn and Bianca were already there, standing among the other six hot-air balloons now resting on the ground. Five were in a circle, one was in the center, and all the chutes were partially deflated.

"Look," said Bianca. "This one's mine!" She was next to a balloon with a pink-and-purple chute. Inside the balloon's basket was a seat labeled with her name.

Gil found his name on the seat inside the basket of the gold-and-orange balloon. Rocky's, in the silver-and-black. Thorn's, in the green-and-gold. Lavinia's, in the blue-and-red.

The sixth balloon, the white one in the middle with a big, green GOLLY printed on it, had an unmarked seat with five oddly shaped indents.

Bianca handed Gil a card and its envelope. "It was in the Golly one," she said.

Before he got the chance to read the card, Rocky ran up, followed closely by Lavinia.

"We got this," Gil said.

Stunt #5

* * * * * * * * * * *

Each box has a piece that will help you.
Just put it into the right place.
Then buckle yourselves in the seat with your name
to see if you're still in this chase.

"Where are the right places?" asked Lavinia.

"In the white balloon," said Gil. He leaned over to examine the indents. One was definitely the shape of a bowling pin. Gil took one of the pins from the bowling game and nestled it into the depression on the seat back.

Click!

"Did you hear that?" he said. "Must be right. Who has the doll?"

Bianca ran it over. "Where does it go?"

Gil took it from her and placed it in a molar-shaped indent, right in the middle of the seat.

Click!

"I have a flag from Around the World," said Thorn. He popped it in next to the doll.

Click!

Without saying a word, Lavinia clicked in the Strewn game disc next to the bowling pin.

Next to that was the last indent, a tiny one.

"What do you have, Rocky?" asked Gil.

Rocky was squatting, sifting through The Salem Witch Game. He came up with the playing pieces and the dice. He looked at his hand. He looked at the spot. Back to his hand. He flicked away the dice. Looked to the spot. To his hand. He picked up a little cat and tried it in the last space. It didn't fit. He went to throw it over his shoulder, but Gil grabbed his hand.

"Gimme." Gil took it, laid it on its side.

Click!

The white balloon began to vibrate. Its chute started refilling. "Everyone! In your balloons!"

"And Thorn," Rocky said, "just get in and close your eyes."

"No problem," said Thorn.

Gil jumped into his basket, buckled his seat belt. His balloon vibrated. The rest of the chutes sprang to life. They wriggled. Danced. Plumped.

The six balloons rose into the air. Higher. Higher. Higher. The lights went out. Trumpets blared, building and building to a crescendo that ended in one long note as Gil's balloon bumped the ceiling. Fireworks sparked and arced, whistled and popped. Then one word flashed, from the floors, the ceilings, the walls.

WINNERS!

CHAPTER 16

Could Gil's heart pump faster? Could he scream louder? He didn't know, couldn't tell. He wanted out, out of the balloon. He needed to jump. Dance. Celebrate.

Spotlights shone, a floor moved underneath their baskets, railings locked into place. Gil's seat belt automatically unbuckled. He leaped out of the basket. Screamed. Jumped up and down on the platform in the warehouse sky. Hands slapped his back, arms lifted him off his feet. He may have kissed Bianca, or was it Thorn? One minute he was running in circles with Lavinia; the next he was bumping chests with Rocky.

Carol galloped up. Together the team surged toward her, tousling her red curls, enveloping her in a group hug that turned into a group bounce.

When Gil hugged Rocky for the third or the thirtieth time, he realized he was hugging Rocky. He moved away and paced in small circles to catch his breath, punching a few victory fists into the air. He rubbed his jaw to massage his smile muscles. He tried to relax his mouth, but it felt frozen in a permanent grin.

"Aah!" Carol screamed as the trumpets died down. "Time to taste victory. Let's eat." She led the green team from the floor in the sky, jumping along three halls and down four flights of stairs to a dining room with enough food to feed a small nation. "Stand here for a moment and look."

Trays of pizza, hot dogs, hamburgers, chicken fingers, and french fries lined one banquet table. Popcorn, potato chips, tortilla chips, cheese curls, pretzels, salsa, and other dips fanned out on another. The third had platters of salmon, chicken, pastas, salads, fruits, and vegetables. A fourth held cookies, doughnuts, pies, cakes, and a huge chocolate volcano.

In the center of the room, an old-fashioned soda jerk stood behind an antique ice-cream counter. "Dishing up anything you can dream up!" he called. The hand-lettered menu above him echoed that. On one side of him flowed a dazzling fountain of sparkling red punch. On the other, gleaming ice sculptures surrounded a vast selection of sodas, waters, and lemonades.

"Can we eat?" asked Rocky.

"First, welcome our guests." Carol opened the door for the red team. They didn't look giddy, but they weren't mad, either. They must have received great runner-up gifts. Bill, their guide, followed, protecting his hair with his hands. Behind him flowed a rush of adults: Curt. Then Lavinia's mom. Then Gil's parents.

Gil hugged them both. When he finally let go, his dad kept grabbing his shoulders, and his mom kept hold of his hand. He opened his mouth to speak, but felt like anything he said would come out with a gush of tears. "So what'd you think?" he managed to squeak out.

Gil's mom took a long, shaky breath. "You were amazing. A true leader."

"Oh, Mom."

"No, really," she said. "I couldn't have been that patient with some of the personalities you had to work with."

Gil shrugged. Agreed inside.

"I don't know how you figured out some of those puzzles," said his dad. "And when you made that mistake, I nearly lost my mind. The other team had cruised through that puzzle. We thought it was all over and could barely stand to watch."

"How much did we win by?"

"You don't want to know," said his dad. "I'll tell you all about it later, but right now, someone's waiting for you." He led Gil over to Old Man Golliwop.

"Pleased to see you again, sir." Gil shook his hand.

"Young Goodson! You kept your promise," he said. "Now on with you." The old man shooed Gil away with his free hand as he kept waggling Gil's handshake with the other. "Go get yourself some food, and put some skin on those bones. Do it before the other vultures eat it all." Still holding on, he looked deep into Gil's eyes and allowed a tiny smile to creep across his face. "Attaboy," he whispered. He let go and wheeled off.

Gil headed for the food table, his stomach knotting like an overtwisted rubberband. Maybe it was the jitters. Or maybe he was really hungry. He tested his appetite with a pretzel, then he loaded only two plates to save room for some outrageous ice-cream mountain.

He and his parents settled at a dining table away from the food and away from most of the TV cameras. He kept grinning at his mom and dad, who grinned right back. Then they all burst out laughing.

No need to speak. He was here, part of a winning team. Here, fair and square, cameras watching. Gil had beat 24,995 others. Four to go.

He already had bragging rights. No one else in Orchard Heights had gotten this far. No one in the state. Yet underneath his excitement, he felt sort of calm and confident. Things would be different. He would be different. He could walk out of here with his head held high.

No more hiding for him. No more hiding? Maybe he really had withered into invisibility like Frankie had said. Maybe he *had* avoided everyone.

He sighed.

"What's the matter, Gil?" said his mom.

"Nothing. Everything."

His dad nodded. "Lots to wrap your mind around."

His dad always understood. Or maybe his dad had his own set of doubts. Like what if he had agreed with the old man's words that day in the courtroom? What if he had pushed to get his old job back? Or what if they had moved to Phoenix right after the trial?

Gil dug into his half-eaten sundae, but left his spoon in the middle of the ice cream and sauces. He didn't need an overfull stomach *and* waves of what-ifs to weigh him down for the next round.

He excused himself and ducked into the bathroom, turned on a faucet and plunged his hands under the rush of water. When it reached the perfect heat, he concentrated on the sensation of water bubbles massaging his palms, allowing that calm to radiate up his arms, around his neck, and into his temples. He closed his eyes and tilted his head back and rotated it. Listened to the tension crinkle around his neck then disappear. He took in a calming breath, then another, then—

"Gil Goodson."

Gil snapped to attention. "Yes, Mr. Golliwop?"

Bert Golliwop strode over to him and turned off the faucets. "Have you ever heard of corporate responsibility?"

Gil was only running some water. He hadn't taken the extra candy bars and peanuts from the concession stands like he could have yesterday.

"Well, Gil?" he said like a cranky teacher. "Do you know what that means?"

Gil dried his hands with a paper towel. "A little, sir."

"It not only means we need to make enough money to take care of our fifty thousand Golly employees worldwide, we are also responsible to the millions of everyday people who have invested their money in toys and games."

Bert Golliwop's tone softened. "Now, son, you know this is a happy place. It didn't end so happily for your father, but given what we knew, we had to protect our interests. You may not like that, but you can understand that, can't you? Trying to protect something?"

Gil nodded, wondered if this was leading to the same conversation as yesterday.

"So right now," Bert Golliwop continued, "I have something very important to protect. I have to protect the Gollywhopper Games. When we decided to sink millions and millions of dollars into this little production, we knew we'd get double that amount's worth in exciting publicity. We planned it all out, except we didn't plan on you, an ex-employee's kid."

Gil wanted to escape, but the way Bert Golliwop

was peeking into each bathroom stall, Gil knew he was about to say something important.

"Now, you know how reporters operate. They'll dredge up all that history. You don't want that, we don't want that, and neither do our fans, who expect to turn on their TVs to see a competition but instead find the Ancient History Network. So I have a deal for you. A good one.

"We could say you were in here vomiting or that you splashed water on the floor, then slipped, and sprained your ankle. You couldn't continue, so you gave your spot to the first alternate. You do this, and not only will you walk away with the consolation prize, but I will personally give you a whole wheelbarrow full of money." Mr. Golliwop pulled out a paper towel and dried the sink. "Remember, Gil, this competition is winner-take-all. Even if you come in second, you wouldn't see an additional cent. This is guaranteed money I'm offering, son. Enough to send you to college for four years. Enough to buy you all the electronic gadgets you could want. What do you say?"

Gil squeezed the paper towel he still had in his

hands. That would be enough money to leave town. Start over. That would be . . .

He threw the towel into the garbage. "Are you making the same offer to Rocky?"

"Why would I . . ."

"Ex-employee's kid?"

Bert Golliwop's face turned as red as a cartoon character just before steam whistles out his ears. "Maybe you don't understand the difference," he said in a whole different tone of voice. "Otherwise you wouldn't have dragged your father in here, totally mortifying him, forcing him to face his past offenses. Shame on you."

Shame on him? Shame on him? Gil sucked in some air. "You don't know a thing—"

Bert Golliwop held up a hand. "Oh, I know plenty. Just don't fall into the same trap as your father did. Don't get greedy today. Take the money—"

"So you can come arrest me?"

He dared to laugh. "I'm not having you arrested. I'm insuring your future. I'm the good guy here. Didn't you hear me before?" he said. Then he enunciated every word. "I don't want you in these games."

He took a step closer to Gil. "You can do this voluntarily, or I can find a way to disqualify you. I'm a smart man."

A rushing sound ran through Gil's ears, as if his body were filling with water, threatening to drown his lungs. He grabbed onto the counter and plunged to his knees.

"Perfect. I found you here on the floor. You fainted. You need medical attention. I'll—"

Gil found his legs, rose up. "I'm fine," he said. "And I'm not a quitter." He brushed past Bert Golliwop, backed toward the door. "If you didn't want me in the Games, then you shouldn't have written the rules so I could play." He spun around, pushed through the door, and out into the crowd.

He found his dad walking toward the bathroom. "You were in there so long, I was about to send a rescue . . ." He looked Gil in the eye. "Gil, you're pale. What's wrong?"

"Did I drag you here, Dad? Am I an embarrassment? Are you mortified to be here?"

"You are never an embarrassment. And I'm fine. What's—"

"I don't want to talk about it anymore."

His father looked toward the bathroom door. Bert Golliwop marched out. Smiling.

"What did he say to you?"

Gil shook his head.

"Tell me."

"He wants me to drop out. Said he'd pay me." Gil closed his eyes.

"I swear . . ." His dad took two steps toward Bert Golliwop.

Gil grabbed onto his arm. "Don't, Dad."

He took another step, looked at Gil, then at a TV camera. He touched Gil's elbow, led him away from the cameras, back into the bathroom. "I need you to tell me everything he said."

Gil tried to remember it all, pausing to let his dad scribble notes on a paper towel.

"What are you going to do with those?" Gil asked.

"I don't know," said his dad. "Maybe nothing, but definitely nothing to ruin the Games for you. I promise." Then he smiled. "You really told him that? How he should've written the rules differently if he didn't want you to play?"

Gil nodded.

His dad laughed, grabbed him up, and hugged him hard. "Bert wanted to rattle you so you'd lose. You need to know that. He's not running the show today. There's a board of administrators from an independent judging agency plus officials from the federal government overseeing the Games. Bert can threaten you all he wants, but he can't disqualify you. So, like I said this morning, throw away the garbage, and go have fun."

CHAPTER 17

Throw away the garbage? During each of the five challenges, Gil had stayed away from the past. He knew he could get into that zone again, especially if the next task involved pummeling anything with a sledgehammer. Picturing Bert Golliwop's face underneath. It would—

"Ready, Gil?" Carol's words brought him back. "Go wait by the door. I'll be right there."

Carol herded the others over one by one until all five were there. "You're in luck," she said, leading them from the dining room. "You get the pleasure of my company till the bitter end."

They continued down several halls and several

flights of stairs until they reached their original conference room.

Carol spoke into her headset. "We're here." She paused, then tapped on the mouthpiece. "Hello?" She took it off. "They can't hear me. Sit tight. I need to switch this out."

The second she slipped out the door, Thorn grabbed Gil's shoulder. "I need my earpiece."

"I don't have it," Gil said. "Never did. You put it into your shirt pocket."

Thorn patted his pocket and shook his head.

"Then it probably fell out," said Gil, walking away.

Thorn jerked Gil's belt loop.

Gil wasn't in the mood. "I told you," he said. "I don't have it."

"I need it," said Thorn. "I know I climbed that tree, and maybe I can succeed by myself, but you don't understand. I can't mess up. They expect me to land on top."

"Sorry," Gil said. "I never had it, but you can check my pockets."

Thorn shook his head and sank into a chair.

"Sorry," Gil said again. And he really did feel sorry

for whatever pressure Thorn was feeling, but he couldn't keep himself from smiling. This would be a fair fight now. Thorn couldn't cheat. Rocky couldn't, either, not with all the cameras. Why weren't there cameras in the bathroom to catch what Bert Golliwop had said to him?

Maybe Bert didn't have control over the Games, but what if he ran to the judges with some horrible lie? What if they yanked Gil off the team? What if—

"Okay, we're ready," said Carol, hustling back, not looking in the least like she was going to eject Gil from the Games.

"Before we go," she said, "I need to emphasize one thing. Remember how you had to come together as a team?" She looked at each one of them. "Well, forget that. You are *not* a team anymore. It's like you were in the Olympics in a five-person relay, if they had such a thing. And now you're competing for individual medals. The only person you can rely on is yourself."

Rocky grinned. Too big.

Fine. Let the cameras catch him cheating.

"In a minute," Carol continued, "you'll go back

into the area you used for the team competition, but don't expect it to look the same. Instead, you'll see five doors. Each leads to a small room. Each room is an exact duplicate of the others. You will not have any camerapeople inside to distract you, but cameras are hidden in the walls and suspended from the ceilings."

Carol looked at the large green watch on her wrist. "Here's the drill. As soon as I stop talking, you'll go in and find the door marked with your name. Stand in front of it, hands to your sides. When you hear the chimes, go into your room, and get to work. The first four of you to complete the task will continue to the next round. I would ask if you had questions, but I'm not allowed to answer them. I can tell you only five more things.

"One, there will be bathroom breaks between rounds. Two, you may leave your room. You have access to every hallway in the entire building. The closed-door offices are off-limits, as are the darkened work areas. Three, the adults who brought you here will be in a viewing area much like before, watching you live and on the TV monitors. Four, I will give you no hints or clues. Unless you're dead, I cannot talk to you until you've completed your task. And five, your task will become apparent once you get inside.

"And I lied." Carol gave her first smile since lunch. "There is a number six. The other team has been sequestered in a lovely viewing area. Once you've been eliminated you, too, will stay in lockdown until the entire competition is over."

"Why can't we leave?" asked Thorn.

"You didn't read all your instructions, did you?" Carol looked down at him. "If we shove you out the door one at a time, the whole world will know who's winning. And you're sworn to secrecy until the network broadcasts the entire competition tomorrow night. Or you lose money. And there might be a messy lawsuit, and, trust me, you want to stay here."

Thorn nodded.

Carol led them, the long way, to the massive green doors. They opened. "Let's go."

Gil did a double take. The hot-air balloons, the giant bowling pin, the palm trees? Gone. He moved to his starting place.

Blong!

He flung open the door so hard, it ricocheted and almost hit him in the face. He caught it and stepped in.

Dead ahead, on thrones, sat two of the most life-like mannequins he had ever seen. One man and one woman, dressed in royal robes of satin and fur, scowled at him.

Gil looked around the rest of the room. The walls, painted a deep blue, matched the tile under his feet. Between him and the mannequins, almost disappearing into the blueness and the shadows, stood a table covered in navy velvet. On it were two items: a miniature version of the personalized treasure chest that had greeted him this morning and a white card.

> Here is something you don't often see:
> A jigsaw puzzle for royalty.
> The king and queen are wearing frowns
> For they've no jewels upon their crowns.
> To brighten up their gloomy faces,
> Put the stones into their places.

Put some jewels into some crowns? No sweat. Then Gil unlatched the treasure chest. Inside gleamed a

jumble of jewels—different sizes, different colors. He snatched up a handful, took a step toward the crowns, and stopped.

What if he dropped a jewel? Better to bring the crowns here.

He returned the stones to the chest and skidded to the thrones to grab the blue-and-green crown off the head of the king. Gil pulled it up, but it wouldn't move, it wouldn't twist. He tried tilting it to the right then to the left. He tugged the crown toward him. It shifted, then caught on something. He slid his fingers between the crown and the head and felt a button. He pushed it, the crown ejected, and he ran it to the table.

Back for the queen's red-and-white crown. He twisted, he pulled, but hers wouldn't budge, and there was no ejector button. In fact, he couldn't get his fingers between the crown and her scalp. They were firmly attached to one another. Maybe her whole head came off.

Gil tugged at her ears and wiggled her earrings. He stuck his fingers up her nose and in her mouth. Then he noticed the two ruby, Frankenstein-type bolts on her diamond necklace. With one hand on each side, he simultaneously unscrewed the bolts. The queen's head wobbled then came off with half her neck.

Gil ran the head to the velvet table. Where to begin? He eased the treasure chest on its side and swept out all the jewels.

He sat at the stool behind the table and started separating the stones into color groups. Wait. Why was he sorting by color instead of size? He picked up a round diamond and tried to find its spot in the white area of the queen's crown. Nope. Only oval holes in hers and round ones in the king's.

Change gears. Sort each jewel by shape. Or should he just slap each one into a crown as he picked it up? Just sort, Goodson. Just beat one person.

Bianca. Poor Bianca. Could she concentrate right now? Or was this like transporting her to King Tut's tomb? Her own personal Disneyland.

Didn't matter. If Gil couldn't concentrate, he'd be gone. And not from this town. "Stop thinking," he muttered, "and—"

He dropped a diamond. He had to stop. Concentrate. Sort without getting sloppy. This was taking so long. So long. Finally. Time to start plugging in the stones.

The front of the king's crown had the largest hole, about the size of a dime. To either side of center were fifteen more holes, each one decreasing in size until they met in the back at a gold crest with the Golly logo. By then, the holes were smaller than a pencil eraser.

Piece of cake. Gil moved the stones around on the velvet work surface, trying to put them in order of decreasing size. Easier said than done. The diamonds stood out most on the velvet background and looked the biggest. The sapphires blended into the deep blue and would have faded away if it weren't for their glimmer.

Tick, tick, tick. Plug them in. Trial and error. Plug 'em in. Make a mistake. Dig 'em out. As the jewels got smaller, Gil's judgment got worse. His fingers had never felt so thick and clumsy. Maybe he'd ruled out Bianca too fast.

Jewel number thirty. In. Thirty-one. In. He was out of holes, but he still had a jewel. Where did number thirty-two go? It was one last ruby, not much bigger than a nail head, and it wasn't a souvenir. Everything had had a purpose. That wouldn't change now.

There had to be another hole. Gil pulled out the center stone. Underneath that? No. Carefully, so carefully, he turned the crown over. Nothing on the inside. Starting with the smallest stone on the left, he counted the holes and stones, rotating the crown with every number. Thirty, thirty-one, then the Golly logo on the back.

Don't lose this here. Think, think. Golly logo. Golly logo.

He brought his head eye-level with the Golly logo. The *O* of the Golly logo. The perfect size for a tiny ruby.

Plink.

On to the queen's crown. Jewel holes in the white part; none in the red trim.

This wasn't that hard, but it was intense. Gil stretched his arms, cracked his neck. Go. Faster. He scooted the stool over and yanked the queen's head toward—

The edge of her neck sent a small pile of oval stones skittering across the floor. He dropped to all fours, spied some of them. He felt around and found two more. "Please, let that be all," he whispered.

He got back on his stool, his fingers shaking. Gil picked up the queen's head more carefully this time.

Deep breath. Back to work. Gil stuck in one oval stone. It glided in. So did the next. The next. The next. Too easy.

He brought the crown closer to his eyes. Closer, closer.

Dots.

Most holes had pinpoint specks of blue, red, or green above them. Some didn't. But the diamonds were clear, and clear wouldn't show up on white velvet. Okay. All right.

Gil dug out the stones he'd put in at random, then replanted each stone to correspond with its speck of color. All the stones, gone. But he still had a hole left.

He was missing a sapphire, a shiny blue stone on shiny blue tile.

His eyes scanned back and forth, but couldn't see the stone. He patted the floor around the table, but all he felt was smooth.

His mind flashed to the time his aunt Katherine had dropped the back of her silver earring on their gray kitchen floor. Gil had laughed so hard when she threw herself, belly flat to the ground, and surveyed the surface at eye-level.

He wasn't laughing now. He was doing the same thing with the same results. He spied the stone inches from the thrones. He grabbed it, pushed it in. Done! Just had to put those crowns back on.

Gil depressed the king's head button and rocked his crown until it clicked. He set the queen's head back onto her neck. He quickly twisted the bolts and . . .

"Yes!"

The faces lit from inside out, and their scowls transformed into smiles.

A click came from behind him. Gil spun around. His door had opened. He peered out. Lavinia was the only other person there.

Gil high-fived Lavinia. High-fived Carol, who took him by the shoulders and spun him halfway around. "There's a lounge over there with plenty to keep you occupied. I was about to send Lavinia, but they told me to wait. You, Gil, were hot on her heels. Anyway, go and relax, be yourselves. Cameras and microphones are banned in there."

Gil pointed to the doors. "Do we get to watch them finish, like on TV monitors?"

"Sorry, Charlie. I'm sure you want to, but we decided it might give you an unfair advantage."

"Why?" said Gil. "We already finished."

"You could learn their deepest, darkest secrets,

their private approaches to puzzle solving, something mysterious and mystic you might be able to use later."

"Got it," said Gil.

"Now on with you to the lounge. I've got work to do."

Lavinia and Gil stopped at the threshold of the three-walled room.

"Wow!"

Lavinia nodded. "This is lovely."

Four blue-leather recliners and a plump sofa with blue and white swirls were arranged in the center of the room on plush navy carpeting. Against one wall, shelves bulged with magazines, comic books, joke books, CDs, DVDs, and video games. The second side had enough personal CD players for all of them, plus wall-to-wall TV monitors hooked to DVD players and Golly GameSystems. A banquet table, pushed against the third wall, sagged with snacks.

Gil grabbed a handful of pretzels. "I knew you'd be my toughest competition," he said.

Lavinia beamed. "I truly believe if our team had been just you and me, we would have finished even faster."

"Probably, but Bianca with her Moonglo makeup . . ."

"True," Lavinia said. "I also suppose Rocky and Thorn had their moments." She reached to her ponytail. Patted around. "Must have lost my ribbon in there. Do you think they'll let me go back? Oh, forget it." She unleashed her hair from its band. "I think I've outgrown ribbons."

"I thought it was just me. But not with the ribbons," he said. "This place makes you feel like you can conquer the world."

Lavinia laughed. "I wonder what they pump into the air. If only we could bottle it and carry it with us." She pointed toward the TVs. "Mind if I see what's over here? We don't have much of this in our home. Join me if you want."

"Go ahead," said Gil. He didn't want to watch or play anything right now. Instead he sank into the blue chair that looked out on the contestants' hallway. He reclined the chair, then tried out one of the buttons on its remote. The seat vibrated. He pushed another and felt fists massage his back. Ahh. He closed his eyes. Someday, somehow, he'd get one of these.

Gil forced an eye open to the sound of footsteps in the hall outside the lounge. Bad time to doze. He shot the chair upright.

Well, hooray for Thorn. He did it himself, without the earpiece.

"Congratulations," he said as Thorn strode into the room. "I knew you could do it."

"I did do it, didn't I?" Thorn lifted his head, almost glowed as he passed Gil's chair. By the time he put some potato chips and onion dip on a plate and came back toward Gil, that glow had fizzled out.

"You don't seem too excited," said Gil.

"I may be on top now," Thorn said, "but it won't last, not without help. I realized that when I had to climb the fake palm tree."

Was he giving up? "What do you mean?"

He sat in a chair next to Gil. "When Rocky was teaching me how to climb? And you were telling me not to look down? It was the first time, probably since I learned to ride a bicycle, that someone bothered to teach me something practical. I have people who are practical for me."

"That doesn't sound bad."

Thorn pointed at his dip. "I mean, I wouldn't know where this comes from. Do you buy it in a container from some store? Do you make it in the kitchen? Does the dip fairy put it in your refrigerator? We have a cook, so I don't know if I could even turn on the stove just to boil water. That's not good. So I doubt I'll win today, but I won't leave as a loser."

Gil wanted to ask Thorn what he meant, but a click down the hall pulled him to his feet.

Rocky bounded out, fists raised in victory like he'd finished first.

Carol came from the shadows and pointed him toward the lounge. His victory prance stopped. He loped into the room. "I could've beaten all of you," he said. "I'm saving up for when it really counts."

Gil looked past him to watch Carol turn the knob to Bianca's room. He braced himself for the drama. Please. No tears, no sobs, no quivering lips.

Bianca glided out with the completed green-and-blue crown on her head. She looked directly into the camera, posed, then burst into laughter. "I guess this means I didn't win," she said to the camera. "But I accomplished my goal. I'm on TV. And I had a great time. Especially with my friend Gil. He's cool. And Lavinia. She can be cool, too. So root for them. And root for me on becoming a model or an actress. Or maybe even a history teacher. Bye, everyone!" She gave a wave then flounced toward the lounge with Carol three steps ahead.

"Incoming cameras," said Carol. "They want to shoot thirty seconds of good-byes."

Bianca fluttered in, then perched on the arm of Gil's chair. "I really mean it, Gil. I'll be rooting for you." She leaned over to give him a hug and plopped into his lap instead. Her crown tipped over, shielding her eyes.

Gil was certain his face had turned a lovely shade of ketchup. He laughed. Helped Bianca struggle back to the arm of the chair.

She steadied herself with a hand on his shoulder. "You know, Double G, I wouldn't have gotten this far without you." She gave him a peck on the cheek, then started to the exit. "And cute hair, Lavinia," she called over her shoulder. "Wear it like that." Then she turned to Carol and pointed to her head. "I love this crown. Can I keep it?"

Carol started to put on her headset, then let it fall back around her neck. "How can I deny you? You look so good in it."

"Thanks. Can I stay in here, too?"

"Nope. Sorry. You get to go to the After Lounge."

"Losers' room? Are there cameras in there?"

"A few discreet ones."

"Good." She breezed toward Bill, who was there to whisk her away.

"So now we're down to four," Carol said. "You have ten minutes to regroup. Get a snack, take your potty break, and I'll be back. All the cameras are gone again."

Gil sank back into his chair, let Lavinia's TV noises overshadow whatever Rocky and Thorn were bickering about.

Ten minutes later as promised, Carol whooshed into the room. "I hate to break up this party," she said, "but it's time to trudge on . . . unless three of you want to concede right now."

They stayed silent.

"No? All righty, then. I'm going to sit right here," she said, plopping onto the couch. "And I need the rest of you to sit tight in one of these chairs for a minute while we go to the next round."

As soon as the others claimed their recliners, the room began to revolve. The open side of the lounge turned into a brick wall, then opened again into another corridor with four polka-dot doors. The room stopped.

"We're here," said Carol. "Same routine. Find your door, wait for the chimes, go inside, and get to work. Bathrooms are still in the lounge. Remember, the building is open to you. I give no other clues. Cameras and microphones are on, but out of your way. That's it. Get up."

They got into position.

Blong!

Gil opened his door. In front of him on the polished wooden floor stood an executive desk and a leather chair on wheels. A camera dipped in from the warehouse ceiling. And the visitor's gallery, above and to the right? Gone.

Yes! No hand signals for Rocky.

Then he heard coughing from above. Above and to the left. Another observation area.

"Okay, Mr. Titus," Gil said under his breath. "It's you against me against Bert Golliwop."

He spun into his chair, swept his hands across the bare desk and opened the drawers, looking for his puzzle. The main drawer contained pens, pencils, a pad of paper, and the same kind of keypad they'd used in the stadium. The drawers to his right were empty, but the one on the bottom left held a tall, thin, folded card. The front read "Xenia's Café" in old-fashioned script. Gil opened it.

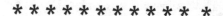

Thaddeus G. Golliwop's favorite uncle Ebenezer was a most peculiar man with most peculiar eating habits.
He loved almonds, but wouldn't eat walnuts.
He loved eggplant, but wouldn't eat yellow squash.
He loved ice cream, but wouldn't eat sherbet.
He loved olives, but wouldn't eat pickles.
He loved Ugli fruit, but wouldn't eat grapes.

One day, sixty-five years ago, the two of them went to Xenia's Café for lunch, but Uncle Eb forgot his glasses and couldn't read the menu.

"Tad." (That was his nickname for young Mr. Golliwop.) "Tad," he said, "you know what I like. Go ahead and place our order while I run back to the house for my glasses. I'll need them later."

Young Tad looked through the menu and ordered all the things his uncle liked. Then for himself he ordered a ham sandwich, a glass of milk, and an ice-cream sundae.

By the time Uncle Eb returned, the food was on the table. "This is perfect for me, Tad. But I don't know how you can bring yourself to drink milk and eat that ham sandwich."

* * * * * * * * * * *

HERE'S YOUR QUESTION:
WHAT WAS THE TOTAL AMOUNT OF
THEIR LUNCH BILL?
(Include neither tax nor tip.)

* * * * * * * * * * *

OTHER IMPORTANT INFORMATION:

When you've reached your answer, enter that amount into your keypad. Again, the keypad will not function as a calculator. This time, though, if you enter an incorrect amount, you will receive an error message. Try again. You will, however, be issued a two-minute penalty for each error. Good luck.

* * * * * * * * * * *

First thing, find a menu. No way to know what Uncle Eb would order without a menu. Gil flipped over the puzzle, and there it was. Sort of.

* * * * * * * * * * *

TODAY, XENIA'S CAFÉ WILL SERVE

Applesauce	Fish of the Day
Baked Chicken	Garden Salad
Coffee	Ham Sandwich
Dumplings	Ice-Cream Sundae
Eggs, Any Style	Jelly Doughnut

Kidney Pie	Soup du Jour
Liver and Onions	Tea
Milk	Upside-Down Cake
Navy Beans	Veal Cutlet
Orange Juice	Whipped Potatoes and Gravy
Pork Chops	Xenia's Famous Layer Cake
Quince Pie	Yams
Roll and Butter	Zucchini

* * * * * * * * * * *

So here was the food, but where were the prices?

Gil scanned the walls. Still bare. He removed the desk drawers to see if they'd hidden the real menu somewhere inside the desk's shell. Nothing. He dropped to the floor and looked underneath the desk. No. He flipped through the legal pad. Nothing written there, either.

Breathe. Think. Breathe. Think.

Okay. Carol had told them twice. The building was open to them. *The building.* Books in the conference room. Magazines in the lounge. Two places to search.

Gil spun around. Grabbed the doorknob. Heard some coughing from above. Spun back and sat at the desk. Those prices were worthless until he knew what Tad ordered.

Gil stared at the menu, willing Uncle Eb's choices to pop out at him. He reread the instructions, but discovered nothing else. He wrote down what he knew.

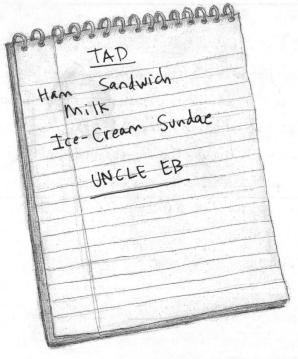

Gil tapped the pencil eraser on the desk. "Uncle Eb," he said, half to himself, "tell me what you like to eat. Why almonds, not walnuts? And what in the world is Ugli fruit? I wish you liked grapes. I know grapes, but that doesn't matter right now. It matters why you like some foods and not the others. That's the key."

Tap, tap, tap. Gil looked at his pencil. No key on there. *Tap, tap, tap.* The key had nothing to do with the color of the food or its texture. *Tap, tap, tap.* The key didn't care how many letters or syllables each food had, either.

Gil stared. And stared. And stared. Until the letters looked like hieroglyphics.

He flipped back to Xenia's menu. Tried to picture himself there, watching over Tad. The waitress comes over. "What can I get you to drink?"

"Milk," says Tad. Then he points to the empty seat. "My uncle will want . . ."

Want what?

Gil pictured Tad looking at the menu choices. There was coffee. Then milk farther down, but Uncle Eb hated milk. Orange juice in the next column. And was that all? No. There was tea. Anything else?

Stupid menu. Didn't have a beverage category like normal menus. Even McDonald's—

Wait. This wasn't a normal menu. This was a Golly menu. And . . . so obvious! Alphabetical order. The menu ran from applesauce to zucchini, not skipping a single letter.

Now, find the pattern. Find Uncle Eb's pattern. Gil's heart pumped. He was close. Find the pattern. Find the pattern.

He turned to Uncle Eb's list and scribbled it on the yellow pad.

HE LIKES
almonds
eggplant
ice cream
olives
ugli fruit

HE DOESN'T
waln

Oh, yeah! The initial letters lit like fireworks. Uncle Eb ate only vowel foods. But what about the Y? "Uncle Eb! Yes! You don't like yellow squash."

Gil flipped back to the menu and finished writing their order.

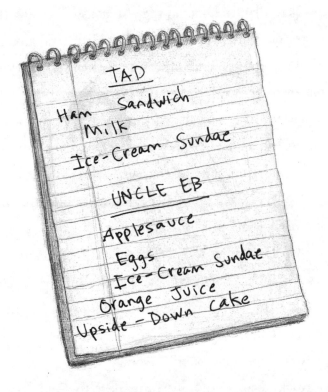

Who'd eat that lunch? Obviously Uncle Eb, but that wasn't Gil's problem. Paying for it was.

Gil raced out of his room, toward the lounge, to the books and magazines.

"What the . . . ?" It wasn't that the magazines weren't there, the lounge itself had disappeared behind a brick wall.

Okay, Plan B. Diner in the warehouse. Through the huge double doors, into the atrium. He turned around. He'd come out through the red doors this time. With his own personal cameraperson following him, he moved to the green pair and shoved through. No warehouse. Just a small, bare room. Its only other door led to their original conference room.

Plan C for conference room. Books on the shelves. What books? They were gone.

Plan D. Dining room. Out the green doors to the atrium. Then down the long hall. Run. Run and think. If he turned where this hall dead-ended, then up four floors, he'd—footsteps behind him.

Rocky and his cameraperson.

Rocky caught up, got right next to Gil's ear. "I knew I'd find you here," he said in a low voice, as if he didn't want the microphones to hear.

"How?" Gil whispered. This was personal, not for TV.

"We have our ways."

Gil's blood rose. He ran faster to keep it pumping to his legs. Forget Rocky. Forget Rocky's dad. Mind on task. Mind on task. If the dining room's empty, Plan E. Plan E. The walls! He had forgotten to look at the artwork and documents on the walls. He'd be coming back that way. He'd look if necessary.

Necessary. He stopped in the barren dining room for three seconds to catch his breath. Great. This reminded him of scenes from spy movies. One minute, the hero's in a room filled with incriminating evidence, but when he returns with the cops, the place doesn't exist anymore.

He inhaled again, then sailed back down the stairs, back down the halls, tuning out Rocky's thuds. Looking right, looking left, looking at portraits of people and toys and games. Looking at nothing that could help. But where were the documents he'd seen earlier? Where? Not on the long walk from the conference room to the warehouse. Before. What was before?

Arrows! Blinking green arrows in the floor, from the entrance to the conference room! Which way?

Which way? Back to the conference room. Start there, trace the arrows backward.

Gil sped back, losing the cameraperson, but unable to shake Rocky and his. Fine. If Rocky wanted to play follow the leader, he'd always be a step behind.

That's why Gil had to keep thinking as he ran. What if the green arrows had also disappeared? No. They'd be there. They had to be. He had no Plan F yet.

C'mon arrows. Be lit. Be lit. Be lit.

Arrows! Blinking! He followed them back toward the entrance. The stuff on the walls didn't help, but what about the trunks they weren't allowed to open before? "There will be a time and a place and a purpose for everything," the welcome card had said. Well, if this wasn't the time, then the time would never be right.

Gil heaved in a breath. Just one more hall, around this corner, and . . . "Aah!" Gil leaped aside, avoiding a major crash with Lavinia and her cameraperson.

She didn't stop, just headed the opposite way with something in her hand.

Good news and bad news rolled into one. Again, she was ahead of him, but Rocky was one step behind. Still, Mr. Titus probably knew what to do

next. Gil had to add faster than— No! The specta-
tors probably had a copy of the menu with the
prices! Fine. Gil could add and run. Add and run.

Gil reached the entrance clogged with more camerapeople. He unlatched the lid of his trunk and
threw it open. Fanned out on top were about ten
crisp one-hundred-dollar bills. Those would keep.
The sheet next to them wouldn't. The Xenia's Café
menu. This one had the prices. He snatched it up,
threw down the trunk lid, started running again,
then took a sideways glance.

Rocky held the menu in one hand and fanned
himself with his thousand dollars in the other. He
ran alongside Gil. "You don't know what kind of
thieves they allow here," he said in full voice. Then
Rocky sped ahead.

Gil could read fast and he could run fast, but not at
the same time. The reading would have to wait. He
shifted gears, found some wind, and chased after Rocky.

He was just two steps behind when he reached his
door. But his breath was coming so fast, he couldn't
stop, couldn't sit, couldn't see. He started coughing.
And heard more coughing.

He. Managed. A. Deep. Breath. More coughing. From him? No. Coughing. From above. Weird coughing. Starts and stops. Mr. Titus.

Click!

Maybe Lavinia's door. Hopefully Lavinia's door.

Click!

Rocky.

Just as long as it wasn't Thorn. It couldn't be, not unless he found his—

No. Gil had to be the third one. He looked at the prices on the menu. Filled in the list:

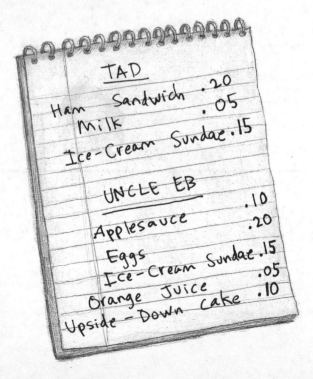

TAD

Ham Sandwich .20
Milk .05
Ice-Cream Sundae .15

UNCLE EB

Applesauce .10
Eggs .20
Ice-Cream Sundae .15
Orange Juice .05
Upside-Down Cake .10

He added it up—two times, three times. He punched a single measly dollar into his keypad. All this for a dollar. But the keypad sparkled with flashes of light. Then it went dark.

His door opened.

Had he missed the *click*? Or had Carol opened it?

Carol stood right outside his door, talking into her headset. Good news or bad news?

"Carol," Gil said.

She held up a finger and mumbled into her microphone.

Should he go to the lounge? Wait here? He took a step toward the lounge. Couldn't see anyone. Another step. Nothing. Another.

"Gil! Sorry."

Sorry she had made him wait, or sorry he lost? He couldn't bear to ask. He tried to smile. "C'mon," she said. "Be happy. You did great. As far as we can tell, you figured out the answer first."

"I'm the first one done?"

She put a hand on his shoulder. "Naw. Third."

"But you said—"

"Lavinia didn't take her camera guy on a wild-goose chase. She knew right where to go for those prices. And Rocky. Darnedest thing. It didn't look like he was thinking much, but there must be lots running around his head that we don't know about. Now I've told you enough. Off to the lounge with you. Catch your breath. I need to deliver the bad news to Thorn."

Gil brushed past Rocky, who was standing at the snack table, and went over to Lavinia.

She sat cross-legged on the floor, playing a video game. She looked up at Gil. "One moment," she said. She inched her hero along, trying to help him avoid danger. He died. "I can't quite get the hang of this." She flashed him a genuine smile.

"But you got the hang of that last puzzle," Gil said. "Congratulations."

"It was exhilarating, wasn't it? Exactly what I'd hoped for when I entered the Games. A real puzzle with a real question. I hope they—"

"Incoming cameras," Carol yelled. "The thirty-second good-bye."

Thorn went around the room, shaking hands. He thanked Rocky for the climbing help, Lavinia for asking his opinion, and Gil for not getting mad when he messed up the doll's toes. "One more thing, Gil," he said. "All that talking earlier? Thanks for not laughing."

"No problem," said Gil.

Thorn smiled, then went with Bill.

Gil grabbed a bottle of water from the table and claimed his recliner. He stared into the ceiling. No crowd. No cameras. Just him and—

Rocky thudded on the arm of his chair, popping peanuts into his mouth.

Gil groaned. "What do you want?"

Rocky wiped his hands on his pants and pulled the hundred-dollar bills from his pocket. "It's like this," he said, fanning himself with the money. "I was just thinking . . ."

"Didn't know you could."

"Very funny, Gil. Anyway, this thousand dollars? If losers get this, I wonder what winners like me will get."

"There's no guarantee you'll win."

Rocky grinned. "I'm about to pull out my guarantee. You just wait."

Gil wanted to plug his ears. Instead, he pulled on the reclining lever and dug his heels into the footrest, pushing down as hard and fast as he could.

The recliner shot upright, and Rocky spilled from its arm.

"Sorry," said Gil. He grinned down at Rocky, and went over to watch Lavinia play her video game until Carol breezed back in.

She sat on the couch next to Rocky. "Grab a chair, Lavinia, Gil. We're going for another ride."

The room revolved again, the open end replaced by a red wall, an orange one, then yellow, green, blue, and purple until it fully opened to what Gil thought would be the warehouse. It had to be the same one, but it didn't look the same. All the props were gone, and in their place? An indescribable brilliance.

Spotlights shone on an enormous complex of translucent walls and windows, sending multicolored rays of light streaming from floor to ceiling, dancing from here to there and back again. To say that they were in the middle of a rainbow could only begin to explain the illusion.

"All right," said Carol. "You guys look like frogs catching flies. You need to close those traps, focus on me, and pay attention. First, forget this is the most breathtaking sight you've ever seen. I'll grant that's impossible, so look at me instead. I'm not as hypnotizing. C'mon. Focus here." She pointed to her face. "Good."

"So, this time, we have three doors that put you each at the starting point of a maze. You are going to love it. And that's all I have to say except everything's fair and square. Each maze is exactly the same and . . ." She held up a finger, spoke into her headset, then pulled it off. "They need one more minute. Hang loose."

Gil turned toward Lavinia, but Rocky grabbed his elbow and pulled him back a couple steps. "Ready for my guarantee?" he said.

"Can't wait," said Gil.

Rocky cupped his hands around his mouth and leaned over to Gil's ear. "Your dad's not guilty."

"I know," Gil said. "I heard the verdict at the trial."

"No," whispered Rocky. "What I mean is, there are people who know your dad didn't do it. I think they might even know who did."

Gil felt the color drain from his face. "Who? You gotta tell me. Who?" He grabbed Rocky's arm.

Rocky tugged away.

"You're lying," said Gil. "It's your guarantee."

"Maybe. Or maybe I do know something."

Gil tried to follow Rocky to his door. Felt a push at his back. Might have heard Rocky wish him luck in the maze. Might have nodded when Carol asked him if he was all right.

Blong!

Gil froze. Squeezed his eyes closed. Shook it off. Rocky's guarantee? Rocky's guarantee would have to wait. Gil had been dealing with The Incident for eighteen months. Maybe for nothing. Rocky was going down. Rocky's dad, down. Gil swung the door open. Took one step in, then stopped in his tracks to grab the dangling white envelope. He ripped it open.

The words danced in front of his eyes. Focus. He shook his head. Focus. He read.

* * * * * * * * * *

WELCOME TO THE
RAINBOW MAZE

Weave in and out and in and out
and up and down and round about.
You'll see so many paths to choose—
from reds and yellows, greens and blues.
Unless you want to pay the price,
be sure to follow this advice:
In roaming through the Rainbow Maze,
heed all the color wheel ways.
For if you don't, you'll doubtless find
that you've been left way far behind.
BUT . . .
Don't go too fast, don't move too quick.
On each right path, you'll find a stick.
For each you hold when you are done,
We'll take five seconds off your run.

* * * * * * * * * *

Gil breathed in. Looked back at the paper.
Okay. He could do this. Concentrate. Fact one.

This was a maze. Fact two. Gil needed to find his way out. Fact three. If he collected sticks along the way, it would cut his time. But what did the rest of the puzzle mean?

Heed all the color wheel ways.

What was a color wheel? Colors on a wheel? Steering wheel? Pinwheel? Forget "wheel."

Rainbow Maze. Rainbows. Spectrums. The colors always appeared in order of that guy's name. Roy G. Biv: red, orange, yellow, green, blue, indigo, violet. This might work. Let the colors lead him through the maze.

Gil stood in a green hallway now. He shoved the puzzle into his pocket and ran forward as far as possible, pulling out a stick the size of a thick pencil from a holder on the wall. Here was his first choice. He could walk up three stairs to the blue area on the left or go up the ramp to the orange passage on the right. Closest to green on the spectrum . . .

"Red, orange, yellow, green, BLUE!" Right next-door.

He shot up the three steps toward the blue area

and meandered around a passageway. A stick! He was on the right path. He ran forward, two sticks in his hand. Another choice: violet or yellow. Neither was next to green. Which was closer?

He dug the puzzle and the pen from his pocket and wrote R O Y G B I V. Aah! Both were two colors away. He needed to try a path. Okay. Yellow.

He trotted up a flight of yellow stairs, around the bend, and smacked into a dead end. No stick. It had to be the other way, but why? Did it matter? What if he just ran? Turned around at dead ends? No. Rocky was probably doing that, and Rocky could run faster.

Why violet? Why? He looked at his color choices again. What exactly was indigo? Blue-violet? What if he removed it? He rewrote his color choices: R O Y G B V.

That made things easier. Down the violet path. Stick! Yes! This led to a choice of yellow, green, or red. He took a quick glimpse at the paper. If the letters circled back around, red would be right next to violet. Up the red stairs, three sticks in his hand.

Faster, faster. Make up for the mistake, for the slow start. Faster. Faster. Grab stick number four. Add it to the—

"Aah!"

The four sticks tumbled down a flight of stairs behind him. Each worth five seconds off his time. Gone. Could he get all four back in less than twenty seconds?

No. Forget the sticks. Go! Move twenty seconds faster than Lavinia. Twenty seconds smarter than Rocky. Move. Move. Move.

Gil used every bit of his brain to focus. He ran deeper and deeper into the maze, able to decide quicker and quicker. With each step, the maze grew more spectacular. Shining, glowing, beaming with intense color. He was in a rhythm now. Run, decide, stop, grab sticks. Up the steps, around the bends, down the ramps, up the ramps. Circling. Climbing. Hoping.

Twenty seconds. He had to make up twenty seconds.

His lungs worked overtime. His legs whined for rest. They must have propelled him a mile. Uphill. Just during this puzzle.

Up a green ramp. Up three blue stairs to a violet straightaway. Up half a flight of red stairs and into an orange corridor that looked like it ran forever.

He took step after step through this one passageway, the orange growing even more brilliant. He came to the end of the orange. To his left, violet. To his right, green. Gil looked at his sheet again. They were both two colors away.

A movement caught his eye in the next maze over. Lavinia! She made a tentative right turn. No time to waste.

Green or violet? Green or violet? Violet. Better to make a mistake than stand there like a deer caught in headlights.

Gil bounded toward violet, then stopped. Everything had a logical explanation. So what explained the glow from that junction? What caused the light to radiate stronger than at any other place inside the maze? It concentrated low, then shimmered up and all around.

Low. On the ground. He raced back and looked down. Yes!

The floor at that crossroads wasn't orange. It was yellow, a yellow trap door that shone like rays of a noonday sun.

Gil grasped the golden ring in the floor and pulled it straight up to reveal a sparkling, golden chute. He sat at the edge of the trap door, dangling his feet until they reached the surface. He lowered himself to a small platform. Held on to the sticks. Scooted down. Laid back. *Whoosh!*

Down he went, gliding by multicolor segments with increasing speed. Then the tunnel turned blind black. His body twisted to the left, then lost speed.

"Aah!"

He felt himself plunge. Another twist left. One to the right. A slowing straightaway, another drop drown. He twisted. He turned. He slid faster and faster.

"Yeah!"

This was the best ride of his life, better than any roller coaster, better than the monster slide at the water park. It felt longer and twistier and almost faster, like a downhill speedway without a seat belt, without a seat.

The next spiral almost tumbled him upside down, but he righted in time for a breakneck straightaway, then a turn to the left. Gil started slowing, seeing shadows, then shapes, then the end of the slide.

Out the chute he came, landing on a red square of carpet in a small room, empty except for two other chute ends and two other squares of carpet. No people, no cameras, no doors.

If he had messed up by going down the chute, he was dead meat. But what a ride!

Gil sat for a second to catch his breath, half expecting to hear a "sorry" come over some loud-speaker. Nothing.

Well, he wasn't going to sit there all day. Only one thing to do.

Gil turned around, stuck his head into the chute, and saw what he must have missed in a blink. He crawled three feet back inside, opened the little orange door, and slithered out, feet first, to the sight of Carol and TV cameras. And Rocky, holding sticks.

CHAPTER 20

"**O**ne one thousand, two one thousand, three one thousand . . ." Gil counted to himself. If he could make it to twenty, he'd have a chance.

"Nine one thousand, ten one thousand, eleven . . ." Still no Lavinia.

"Fourteen one thousand, fifte—"

Her door opened. She handed a bundle of sticks to the officials standing there. "I feel like such a fool. Did anyone else miss the orange door?"

"You all did," said Carol. "Then Rocky . . ."

Gil couldn't listen. Could barely breathe. Maybe Lavinia didn't have all her sticks. Maybe she'd dropped some on the slide. Maybe . . .

The officials counted. They conferred. They looked at Gil. "Sorry," said a woman. "We saw you drop those four sticks. If you had only dropped three . . ."

Gil didn't know if she'd let her voice trail off or if he stopped hearing. Less than five seconds. One stick. Or Rocky's guarantee. Guaranteed to work. Guaranteed to rattle Gil enough to pause five seconds.

It wasn't the lost money. It wasn't even the deal with his dad. He'd let Rocky beat him.

Gil leaned over, fists on his thighs.

Carol put a hand on his back and gave him a bottle of water. "You okay, Gil?"

"Dizzy from the slide, I guess."

"You're not the first," she said, walking him to a chair against the wall. "You should've seen me— major brain roll. So sit and de-fuzz before Bill takes you to the After Lounge. Cameras are off you for a few minutes."

With his elbows on his knees, he hung his head. Not fair. He should be exhilarated, energized. Instead, he needed to suck it in and pretend he was. For the cameras. He took a deep breath and looked up.

Lavinia was standing next to him, her eyes glazed with tears. "I wanted you and me to be last. I wanted it to be a real contest."

Gil looked over at Rocky. "Win for me, Lavinia. Just beat him." He struggled to his feet and gave her a hug. Then he turned to Carol. "Where's Bill?"

Gil didn't wait for her answer. He spotted Bill lurking outside the door. "Get me out of here," he said, walking past him without stopping.

"This is the worst part of my job," Bill said, catching up with him. "You get so close to the end, and you think, 'What if?'"

Gil nodded. But that wasn't exactly it. No one would understand except his mom and his dad. "Where is this Losers' Lounge?"

Bill gave a chuckle. "Why does everyone want to call it that? The After Lounge is a floor above the spectator area. I'll take you to see your parents. After that, you'll join Bianca and Thorn, and you can watch the action live or from any monitor you want."

Gil nodded. Continued the walk to the spectator area in silence, thankful Bill wasn't trying to cheer him up with happy talk.

His mom and dad were waiting right by the door. Gil hadn't needed a hug like this in a long time. "Sorry," he said, taking a small step back.

"Sorry?" his dad said. "There is nothing, nothing to be sorry about. We're so proud."

His mom nodded, tears streaming from her eyes. "Are you okay?" she managed. "We were so worried. At the entrance of the maze. You froze. Were you sick? Nervous?"

Gil ached to tell them what Rocky had said, but he didn't want to cause a scene right here. Rocky would deny it. "Nervous, I guess," he said instead.

His dad draped a hand on his shoulder. "Don't know if this will make you feel better or not, but I've been thinking about our deal ever since we made it."

Gil looked at him, waited.

"We can start figuring a way to move out of town if you still want. It might be good."

Gil had been waiting for months to hear those words, but they didn't bring even a whisper of relief. Maybe he was too tired, too disappointed. Too angry. Gil tried a smile.

"Yeah," said his dad. "We'll talk about that later."

Bill came up to them and pointed toward a projection on the wall flashing *5:00* off and on before it started counting down. "That's our cue. Say your good-byes. You'll see one another soon."

Gil's dad gave him another hug. So did his mom. "Even if you don't believe it, I couldn't be prouder," she said.

Gil nodded.

At the four-and-a-half-minute mark, Bill escorted him up a flight of stairs to a near replica of the area where his parents were. "There's just one rule we have up here. No talking during the competition. Whispering only. Go ahead in and relax."

Bianca rushed up and threw her arms around him. "Gil, I'm so glad to see you. I mean, I'm sorry to see you, but I'm glad you're here."

Her energy put the first smile on his face. "I guess you can't win 'em all."

"I don't think I can win anything," she said. "At least I've never won anything. But it's sort of cool up here. You see everything. Like when you dropped those sticks? I got so sick to my stomach and—"

"Be back in a minute," Gil said. He couldn't take

a play-by-play right now. He went over to Thorn, who was sitting with his back to the Games. "Hey."

Thorn handed Gil a piece of paper.

1. Where does onion dip come from?
2. How do you make grilled cheese sandwiches?
3. Where can I learn to climb?
4. How do my clothes get clean?
5. Who can teach me to bowl?
6. How do you set up a computer?

Gil laughed. Handed the paper back to Thorn.

"At least it's a start," Thorn said. He wrote a number seven.

Gil drifted back to Bianca. "So where's the best place to sit?" he asked.

She grabbed his wrist, pulling him a quarter way around the lounge. "They move the rooms over here so we can see everything. Except for that maze puzzle. We had to use the monitors to see most of it. Are you gonna watch?"

"Yeah," Gil said. "If the next game is a puzzle, I'm

going to try to work it. I need to know if I would have beaten Rocky or Lavinia if I hadn't messed up."

Gil took a stadium seat at the rail and looked down into a pair of muted blue rooms. Each one had a large work desk at the rear, then twenty-five smaller desks, arranged five by five. Those desks each supported a computer monitor with a different screen saver. "When do we get the puzzle?" Gil asked.

Bianca pointed to the arm of his chair. "It's so cute. When the chimes ring, it pops open, and the puzzle's inside."

"Pencils? Paper?"

"On the table back there."

The clock on the wall showed forty-three seconds until the next puzzle.

Gil got something to write with, sat back down, and watched Carol lead Lavinia and Rocky to two doors.

Carol's voice came through speakers in their area. "In a minute," she said, "you'll go through your door and head to the large desk in the back of the room. Your puzzle will be there."

"Yeah," said Bianca. "You get to hear Carol and anyone with her, but if you want to hear Rocky and

Lavinia, you need these headphones." She pointed to a pair near his knee.

He wouldn't be using those. He wanted quiet. And definitely not all this coughing. "Is there any way not to hear Mr. Titus?"

"Is that who it is? He's so annoying," said Bianca. "He was coughing all during the menu puzzle, then I thought he was gone or dead because he was mostly quiet during the maze. But I guess he's back. Prepare to be annoyed."

The cough came again. Carol and Rocky looked up. Lavinia stayed focused on the door.

Blong!

The arm of Gil's chair popped open. He pulled out the puzzle, then shut the arm. He wouldn't look at it yet. Wouldn't look at it until Rocky and Lavinia both got to their desks.

Rocky sat. Ripped open his envelope. Then Lavinia did. Gil opened his.

* * * * * * * * * *

There's much in a name, so they say.
You'll find out without much delay

If you choose the right one
Before you've begun.
Go on now; get ready to play.

Add "pole" to my first name nickname.
Cut my second part short in this game.
Both give you a clue.
Now discount the two,
And mix up the name that remains.

When you've straightened this jumbled-up rhyme,
You've practically finished your climb.
Just choose the right screen
With the right picture scene,
And enter your answer in time.

If Gil were down there, he'd be panicking again. Eventually, he'd push past his pounding heart and sweaty palms, and remember to take this puzzle one step at a time. But up here, he had nothing to lose. He'd never truly know how he would have finished.

Forget it.

He put on the headphones, tuned in to Rocky's

microphone, and looked at the close-up monitor of his desk. He was doodling. Tapping his pencil and doodling. And humming.

Gil switched to Lavinia. She was silent, but she'd written *NAME?* at the top of her paper.

If Gil were doing it, he'd have two names up there: Golly Toy and Game Company and Thaddeus G. Golliwop. This was another company question, the first of today.

Which name would Gil start with?

The puzzle said: *Add "pole" to my first name nickname.* Companies don't have nicknames. People do. Gil would go with Thaddeus G. Golliwop.

"Quwaah. Qua-qua-quaah . . ."

Someone give Mr. Titus a cough drop.

"Qu-qu-qua-kur . . ."

Gil switched the headphones back to Rocky, who stopped humming and started writing some words next to the lines in the poem. His hand, though, blocked what he'd written.

Aah! Gil couldn't just sit there, watching nothing. He grabbed his pencil and listed the pictures on the twenty-five computer screens.

1. Apple tree
2. Pretzels
3. Island
4. Scissors
5. Chef
6. Clock
7. Bowling alley
8. Polar Bear
9. Telephone
10. Tiger
11. Frog
12. Football
13. Art stuff
14. Movie camera
15. Book
16. Dancer
17. Train
18. Pole-vaulter
19. Map
20. Birthday cake
21. Santa
22. Dollar signs
23. Mountain
24. Teacher
25. Candy

By the time he finished, Lavinia had finally written *Thaddeus G. Golliwop* at the top of her page.

Gil wasn't even trying, and he was still one long step ahead of her. He looked at the puzzle again.

Add "pole" to my first name nickname. . . .

Easy. They told him the nickname for Thaddeus in the Xenia's Café puzzle. Tad. Tadpole.

Whatcha doing, Lavinia? It's not Thad. Or Thaddie. Or Deus. Tad. It's Tad.

"Quaah. Qu-quaah. Qu-queeh . . ."

"Will someone please take that man to the hospital?" whispered Bianca.

"Bah-ahchoo. Kah-kah-kah-quoh."

Rocky didn't seem to worry. He wrote more, and the camera, now at a different angle, showed everything.

Next to *There's much in a name, so they say,* Rocky had written: Golly Toy and Game Company = stock market symbol = GOLTAGACO, which made some sense. But the words after four other lines made no sense:

Add "pole" to my first name nickname. First name = GOL + POLE

Cut my second part short in this game. TAGA

Now discount the two, Discount = shorten = POLTAGA

And mix up the name that remains. POLTAGA COMPANY . . . mix it up.

Rocky circled *POLTAGA COMPANY*, then started rearranging some of the letters: *GAC PAPY TAG MAP. MAP!*

"And there he goes," said Bianca.

Rocky popped out of his chair and weaved up and down the rows of computers, looking at each monitor. He paused an extra two seconds at the one with the map from the Octagon Map video game before he returned to his desk.

OCTAGON MAP, he wrote. Then he crossed the corresponding letters from *POLTAGA COMPANY*, circled the *P L A Y* left, then charged out of his seat again, fists pumping in victory.

Gil sank back into his seat. Maybe it was just as well. Rocky wins. Then Gil tells his parents what Rocky said, and maybe they all learn the truth.

Rocky returned to the Octagon Map monitor. He laced his fingers together, turned them inside out, and stretched his arms to crack his knuckles before he sat down like a maestro about to perform a piano concerto in Carnegie Hall.

Mr. Titus started coughing again, but the sound was coming out in sharp barks instead of syllables.

Rocky shook his head and poised his fingers on the keyboard. All he had to do was type his answer, then bells would chime and alarms would ring and the heavens would open and shine on him, and poor Lavinia would be devastated. She probably thought she'd get this one right.

She was still scribbling on her pad of paper, no clue she might have already lost.

Rocky flashed a full-face grin into the camera and typed *PLAY OCTAGON MAP*. He pressed enter, and the screen flashed. The Octagon Map logo reappeared at the top half of the screen. The bottom read:

```
PLAY OCTAGON MAP
STARTING POINT?
```

Mr. Titus's cough came back even sharper.

Rocky casually ran his finger across his throat exactly as he had when Gil had made him tell his dad to quit the signals.

"I know this!" said Rocky. "Get ready, Santa. This is gonna be one monster Christmas in August for me." He typed *NORTH POLE*.

"Kack-kack-kack."

The Octagon Map logo remained at the top, but the bottom half came back with WHO?

"Kack-kack-kack."

Rocky ignored the cough again and typed *SANTA* at the prompt.

"Hey, Gil," whispered Bianca. "How's anyone supposed to know this?"

Buzz!

No trumpets, no light show, no fireworks. The monitor flashed SORRY. TRY AGAIN!

Apparently no one was supposed to know this.

But Gil knew he could still figure out the real answer first. At least he had to try.

He still had *Tadpole* on his paper.

Next: *Cut my second part short in this game.*

The second part had to be the middle name, the name Gil was never excited about, the name written in every annual report. "Thaddeus Gilbert Golliwop."

Gil did what he had done his whole life. He got rid of the Bert and was left with Gil. And tadpoles had gills. This was working.

Now discount the two . . .

Rocky had shortened it. But discount meant something else. Like ignore. Like when the judge said, "Ladies and gentlemen of the jury, please discount the testimony you just heard."

Discount. Make them not count. He drew a box around the two words as if to set them aside, ready to use if he needed them for clues.

What came next? *And mix up the name that remains.*

One name remained: Golliwop. Just one step more. Mix it up and find a real word.

Gil loved anagrams, he was good at anagrams, but his father was better. He wrote *GOLLIWOP* in the space below the discounted words.

TADPOLE

GIL(LS)

GOLLIWOP

It was so simple, so simple . . . if all the letters were there. He wrote down *P*, then crossed the *P* out of *Golliwop* to make sure he didn't use the same letter twice. Then he wrote the *O* and *L* and crossed them out. The other *L*. The *I*. *W*. Another *O*. And the *G*.

Bingo! Tadpole. Gills. Polliwog.

Gil looked down. There. It's there, Lavinia. The screen with the frog. C'mon, Lavinia. It's *polliwog*. The answer's *polliwog*. Go. Type in—

"Ladies and gentlemen! Ladies and gentlemen!" A voice boomed over the speaker system. "We're having major technical difficulties. Please hold tight. We'll be back in a minute."

The monitors in the viewing area went blank. So did the computer screens down below.

Carol hustled to Rocky's room; Bill to Lavinia's. Then Carol and Bill whisked both players out of sight. Fast.

Moments later, Bill whipped through the door, alone, and motioned Gil, Bianca, and Thorn to come closer. "Let me tell you what's going on," he said. "There was an irregularity in this puzzle."

"Like Rocky's answer?" asked Bianca. "That was so bizarre."

"I'm not sure of the specifics," Bill said, but if eyes could speak, his agreed with Bianca. "Anyway, we have backup plans. Carol is on her way with the official announcement and with your other two teammates. Sit tight, and we'll let you know what's going on as soon as we can."

Gil tried to imagine what that meant. Maybe a

computer glitch like at the stadium? Maybe Lavinia and Rocky had received different versions of the puzzle? Maybe before the maze . . .

The lounge door opened. Carol let Lavinia and Rocky into the room. "We need a few more minutes," she said, and she ducked back out.

Bianca marched up to Rocky. "What was that weirdness? Even I knew it didn't make sense."

Rocky looked at her like she was nuts. "I don't know what you're talking about."

"You do, too," said Gil. "Santa. North Pole."

"I guess you don't own Octagon Map. Great video game."

"No, I don't own Octagon Map."

"Well," Rocky said, keeping his stare level, "you have to pick a starting point, and the demo mode starts at the North Pole."

"Does not," said Thorn, coming around. "It starts in Quito, Ecuador, on the equator."

"Maybe I have a different version."

"There is no different version."

If Gil wasn't going to get answers, he didn't need to hear their verbal volleyball. He went over to Lavinia, who was hunched in a spectator seat, still as a statue. "You okay?"

Her fingers gripped the railing. "I don't know what happened. That last puzzle was hard, but I was so close when they stopped us." She looked up at Gil. "Do you think I have another chance?"

"Who knows?" Gil sat next to her and stared down at the computer rooms, which were now revolving out of sight, leaving a bare warehouse floor. He drummed on the railing, tapped his toes. Tried to keep any ray of hope from creeping into his veins. Tried to stop—

"Good news, green team." Carol dashed in.

Dreaming of a second chance?

"You're all going back down. One puzzle. Our first emergency tiebreaker. Winner-take-all. Maybe a bonus for some. That's all I can say. Follow me." Carol started walking.

"That's all you can say?" said Bianca, echoing Gil's thoughts.

Carol stopped and turned around. "Sorry. That is absolutely all I can say. Except, if you want, you may choose not to play." She walked out the door with the five of them following her.

Bill fell into step, but then he put an arm around Rocky. "This way, pal." They peeled off, down a different hallway.

"Where am I going?" said Rocky. "What'd I do? What'd Gil tell you? I wasn't listening to my dad just now. Honest. I was . . ." His voice trailed off.

"Where is he going?" asked Bianca.

"Rocky won't be joining you," said Carol.

Gil just smiled.

"Why?" Bianca said.

No reaction from Carol.

"Carol," she said. "You have to tell us something."

Carol stopped again. "I can tell you to get your minds back into the Games. That's my last word until I give you instructions."

Except for their footsteps, it was silent. Gil thought he could hear the blood rush through his ears. That should have made him feel alive, but the sensation made his heart beat faster. He couldn't let himself get too excited or his palms would sweat even more. He dried his hands on his jeans. If he would've done that before the maze . . . *Would. Could. Should.* Those words never changed results. Only he could change results.

Carol led them back into the contestants' lounge, back to the blue recliners. She looked at a sheet of paper, then lowered it to her side. "I know this must seem very strange," she said. "This afternoon has been no skip in the park for us, either." Then Carol read from the sheet, "'But it appears there may have been a bit of impropriety surrounding the last few rounds.'"

"What's impropriety?" asked Bianca.

"Impropriety," said Carol. "Something not proper."

"You mean fishy?" Bianca said. "Like North Pole and Santa Claus?"

"I need to read this from the sheet. That's all they'll allow me to do. Okay?"

Bianca nodded.

Carol looked back at the paper. "'In a few minutes, the four of you will be led to your doors. When the chimes sound, follow the instructions provided to you. That's all.'"

"That's all?"

Carol smiled, tight-lipped. "Let's go."

They stopped in the hall with the four polka-dot doors they'd used for Uncle Eb.

Gil focused on the gold doorknob, how it reflected the gleam of the lights above. How—

Blong!

Gil grasped the knob. Stormed in. White walls. Brown desk. Computer. Black chair. With one movement, he pushed the mouse and sat. The screen popped to life.

* * * * * * * * * *

```
If you've paid the closest attention

to each puzzle, each hint, and each clue,

then you should glide through every one of the tasks

this computer's presenting to you.

The solution to each of these riddles

is a product, a toy, or a game.

Your aim is to click on the number

sitting next to the right answer's name.

Again, you must race hard to finish;

get started—there's no time to slack,

For if you're not one of the first of two done,

watch your screen slowly fade off to black.
```

* * * * * * * * * *

Gil scrolled to a list of fifty Golly toys and games. They'd be no help now.

* * * * * * * * * *

Puzzle A

Patric Gordo said give, Peter one card

* * * * * * * * * *

Did that mean: "Patric," Gordo said. "Give Peter one card" or was Patric Gordo the first guy's name? And where were the quotation marks, and why was there a comma between—

Wait. The Salem Witch Game. It reeked of the Salem Witch puzzle and its misplaced comma. Answer, two words, split at the comma. First initials. PGSGPOC. That didn't work. Still, this was so much like Salem Witch with its capitalized . . . Wait. The first initials weren't capitalized here.

This puzzle had a new key. Okay. Analyze. First word, first. Patrick without the *K*. Then Gordon without the *N*. Why would they turn common names into weird names and leave out the last letters?

Last letters in each word.

Gil pulled out a pencil and pad of paper from the drawer and wrote the last letters in each word: C O D E , R E D. Bingo!

He scrolled up to the list and double-clicked number 15, Code Red.

The computer highlighted it in blue, but didn't do anything else to show if he was right or wrong. Didn't matter. He was right.

Go. Scroll.

* * * * * * * * * *

Puzzle B

His recipe called for a carrot,

codfish, and cheese.

* * * * * * * * * *

Which puzzle was this? What was the second team puzzle? First was Salem Witch and the piñatas. Then another puzzle and stunt. Palm trees? No. Something before. Island was with the palm trees. That huge doll was fourth. Hot-air balloons, fifth.

Gil jotted those down while he remembered them. But what was puzzle two? Think. First Thorn got that goo on his shirt and complained. Then he . . . he . . . he couldn't bowl. Bowling!

Find the product spelled inside the sentence. Not between the first two words. Not the second and third. Not, not, not.

Maybe this was a backward version, too. He started at the end of the sentence. Nothing between the last two words. Not the second and third to last. Not the . . .

Yes! Backward between the carrot/codfish combo. Doctor.

Gil scrolled to the list. All right. Doctor, Doctor. Number 16.

He clicked it.

Next.

```
* * * * * * * * * *
       Puzzle C
Of brains and muscle,
 spirit and integrity—
  Gollywhopper Games
18, 4, 30, 23, 52, 13, 26, 40, 47, 22, 9, 2

   * * * * * * * * * *
```

No problem. Gil knew what to do. He counted the letters of the haiku until he reached eighteen and wrote *S*. Now the fourth letter. *R?* That couldn't be right. No word begins *SR*. . . .

Okay. Switch it around. Eighteenth from the end of the haiku, the *Y* in *integrity*. And the fourth letter from the end was *A*. And the thirtieth? *T*.

Gil looked at the list. No Golly toy or game started

with those letters. How else could he turn this around? How else? How else? Maybe the numbers were in reverse order.

Gil started at the end of the number chain. Two. *F.* Nine. *A.* Okay. Twenty-two. *I.* Forty-seven. *R.* This seemed to be working, but so many numbers to go. So much counting. Back to the list. Only two choices started with *F.* Only one had twelve letters. *Fairydusters.* He clicked number 19.

* * * * * * * * * *

Puzzle D

Call NEVENS.

* * * * * * * * * *

The Wonder Tiny Dolls clone. But not. No numbers. Just letters.

Gil looked around the room. No phone. No problem. He'd recreate the phone's numbers and corresponding letters on paper.

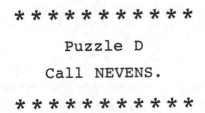

No, no, no. *One* in Wonder Tiny Dolls. That was the trick. One doesn't have any corresponding letters. Neither does the zero. Eight numbers, twenty-six letters. Three letters each. Two left over.

The old trivia question. What two letters don't appear on older phones? Q and Z. But they weren't asking that. He wrote down the list:

2   ABC
3   DEF
4   GHI
5   JKL
6   MNO
7   PQRS
8   TUV
9   WXYZ

Now, call who? NEVENS. He translated the name into numbers. 638367. Numbers don't spell, like Rocky said earlier. So how should he turn this puzzle around?

He wrote down the letters that corresponded to NEVENS' numbers:

```
6  M N O
3  D E F
8  T U V
3  D E F
6  M N O
7  P Q R S
```

Which Golly products started with *M*, *N*, or *O*? He scrolled to see his choices. He had eight of them. Three with six letters in the first word of their names: Melody Magic, Meteor Strike, Olivia the Octopus.

Gil glanced at the numbers and letters. One obvious choice. He checked it number by number to make sure.

```
6 -  M
3 -  E
8 -  T
3 -  E
6 -  O
7 -  R
```

Oh yeah! He clicked that. 24, Meteor Strike.

One last puzzle. Fast. Faster than two of the others still in this. Faster, so his screen wouldn't fade to black. It wouldn't. It couldn't. He'd make it in the top two. But would he make it faster than Lavinia?

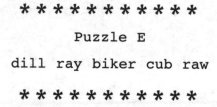

```
* * * * * * * * * *
      Puzzle E
  dill ray biker cub raw

* * * * * * * * * *
```

A flurry of words. Around the World and Back Again. But what was the twist this time? What did he need to reverse?

Could it be that easy? Could the words be in reverse order?

He wrote them that way: raw cub biker ray dill.

Said them out loud. "RawCUBbikERrayDILL. RawCUBbikERrayDILL." Removed the duplicate sounds from between the words. "RawCUBike-RAYdill. Rawk. Rawk." Forget it. Gil looked at the *R*s on the list.

Rock-a-bye Cradle. Number 31.

Heart pounding, hands sweating, he clicked it.

His screen went to black. Did two others finish before him? Was he out again? Did Thorn replace his earpiece? Did—

No! None of that. The screen popped back to life:

```
* * * * * * * * * *
Congratulations!

15 CODE RED

16 DOCTOR, DOCTOR

19 FAIRYDUSTERS

24 METEOR STRIKE

31 ROCK-A-BYE CRADLE


15 16 19 24 31 . . .


What's the next number in the
sequence? Just the number. When you
discover the answer, go directly out
your door and find the cubbyhole
that corresponds to that number.
* * * * * * * * * *
```

15, 16, 19, 24, 31.

Each number was higher than the one before.

Could it be that easy? Fifteen plus one equals sixteen. Sixteen plus three equals nineteen. Nineteen plus five . . .

Plus one. Plus three. Plus five. Plus seven next? Yes! So thirty-one plus—

Gil jumped from his seat, threw open the door, and was faced with a wall of numbered cubbyholes, each big enough to hold a backpack. Another wall of cubbies sat to his left. Forget those. Find number 40. Number 40. Where was 40?

Lavinia's door flew open. She ran out.

Forget her. You're there. You're almost there. Number 40. Number 40. Numbers one through ten across the bottom. Forty. All the way to the right. To the right. Four rows up.

Number 40.

Gil looked in. Nothing but a button. He pressed it.

CHAPTER 22

The ground at Gil's feet rocked like the whole building was about to tumble down. He reached for the cubbies to hold him steady, but they began to move apart and away from him. He stepped back, back against his door. Grasped onto the knob.

Was the floor below him rotating, or was it the wall in front? Had he set off this quaking or did Lavinia?

Dead ahead, crystal rays of light beamed through the space between the cubbies. As the rays grew larger and brighter, the rumbling grew stronger, stronger, stronger, but the floor seemed to have stopped moving. A pathway before them lit, and Gil

and Lavinia walked along it, toward the brilliance, stepping into the blaze of light together.

Had he won? Or had Lavinia? Was it Gil or Lavinia? Gil or . . .

Boom-bah-boom. Bah-bah-BOOM! The woman beating on timpani drums stopped with a flourish. Her podium moved backward between rows of an orchestra that struck up a fanfare.

Gil looked at Lavinia. "Who won? You or me? You or me?"

She shook her head. "I suspect it's—"

The fanfare stopped. Mr. Golliwop rushed out. Shook Lavinia's hand, pulled her aside, waited for the cameras to gather around.

Gil stood alone, the drums still echoing in his chest. At least he pretended it was the leftover timpani noise. Otherwise, it'd be his heart, about to break through his rib cage. He should've won. It should've been him. Without Rocky, he would've beat Lavinia in the maze. He'd stopped working that polliwog puzzle to watch Rocky and still figured it out faster than Lavinia had. If it hadn't been for Rocky, he would've been . . .

"This young woman," Bert Golliwop finally said into the microphones, "was one of the finest competitors we could have ever hoped for. She showed real . . ."

Hands gripped Gil's shoulders from behind. He spun around. Carol.

She leaned over to whisper in his ear. "How's it feel, champ?"

He jerked his head up, met her eyes. "What?"

"You don't know, do you?" She slung an arm around his shoulder. "Gil. You won."

Gil pointed to Lavinia. "But Mr. Golliwop's talking to her and . . ."

She looked at him. Laughed.

"I won?" He jumped. High. Came down. Grabbed Carol, spun her around, let her go. "I won?" Looked over at Lavinia.

Lavinia was smiling. Smiling big. If he won, then . . . "Why is Lavinia so . . ."

"Happy?" said Carol. "All the mess she went through? We decided she deserves to win an extra ten thousand dollars plus a free college education. It's the least we can do."

Gil would take the least. He'd be ecstatic with the least, but . . . He won!

Seconds later, they shuttled Lavinia out, and all the lights turned onto Gil. So did Bert Golliwop's stare. But this time his eyes were almost smiling.

"And now, without further hesitation, the one, the only champion of the Gollywhopper Games, Mr. Gil Goodson!" He thumped Gil's back and pumped his hand.

"Really?"

"Yes, really." Bert turned and looked directly into the camera. "Now let me tell you about this young man. Something you may not know."

Was he going to drag him through the whole nightmare again?

"Something that attests to his character."

Would he have Gil booted from the building?

"Not many twelve-year-olds could continue being so competitive when they were at such a disadvantage."

Which disadvantage?

"But he fought back. He won. And let's bring out his parents." Bert Golliwop leaned over and spoke closer to Gil's ear. "That sounded weird, unfinished, didn't it, son?"

Gil nodded.

"Don't worry. We're going to tape an explanation, and the network people will insert it."

"An explanation of what?"

"Exactly. Didn't want you to hear it without your parents. Now get excited for the cameras again. You won, Gil! You won!"

So many questions. So many, but . . .

He won! He won! "I won!"

Bert Golliwop shook his hand, patted him on the back. Then he looked Gil in the eye before he turned toward a camera. "Do you know what you've won?"

"Yeah," said Gil. "Those hundred-dollar bills in the trunk, a college scholarship, some toys and games, and—"

"You don't know everything yet." Bert shook his head. "No, son. You have no clue. Fact is—are you ready for this?"

Gil nodded.

"You've also won half the profits from our new video and board games: the Gollywhopper Games. Do you have any idea how much that's worth?"

"Ten thousand dollars?"

Bert Golliwop laughed. "Multiply that times one hundred, son. At least," he said. "Over time, that could make you a multimillionaire."

"A what? A what!" Gil jumped. He ran. He won. He won! Through the door. His parents. Had to tell them.

The orchestra struck up something loud and exciting. He jumped on his dad. Jumped on his mom. The three ended in a heap on the floor. Laughing and hugging. Then standing and jumping. And jumping and jumping. Cameras surrounding. Circling. Backing away. Letting Bert Golliwop in. Even he couldn't ruin this moment.

Bert shook hands with Gil's mom. Gave his dad a pat on the back.

Gil felt his exhilaration giving way to question after question after question. Gil couldn't wait much longer for an explanation. "Mr. Golli—"

Bert Golliwop turned away from Gil, toward the cameras. "I'd like to present Gil's parents, Elizabeth and Charles Goodson. And the four of us will be back in few moments."

A woman with a headset and clipboard ran up.

"Bert. Hold on. We need to interview him now. Otherwise, we can't get this on the air tomorrow night."

"Then work half an hour faster, Lara." Bert Golliwop glanced at Gil, then back at the producer. "You already know more than they do. It's only fair."

"Then we're coming in."

Bert Golliwop looked at her with those eyes of stone. "No." He took a deep breath and turned to Gil and his parents. "Now, I need the three of you to follow me." He turned around. "And no one else."

They walked in silence until they'd long cleared the cameras and stepped into the elevator. "What's this about, Bert?" Gil's dad asked.

"Why don't you ask your son?"

"Gil?"

Gil looked at Bert Golliwop. "I didn't do anything wrong."

"No, son, you didn't." The doors of the elevator opened, and Bert Golliwop led them through the eighth-floor hall and into his corner office overlooking the heart of Orchard Heights. "Tell them, Gil. Tell them what made you freeze before the Rainbow Maze."

"You heard that?" Gil said.

Bert Golliwop took a seat behind his desk. "Unless you were in the bathrooms, the lounge, or the conference room, we heard everything. Tell him, Gil."

"I didn't want to tell you before, Dad," Gil said. "Rocky could've been lying to make me lose. I was going to tell you afterward and . . ."

"What, Gil?"

Gil opened his mouth. Couldn't get the words out.

Gil's dad thumped his palms against the back of a leather chair. "Bert. You can see my son's uncomfortable. The facts. Now."

Bert Golliwop looked at Gil's dad. "Rocky said there are people who know you are innocent, said it like he had some information. That's what he told Gil before the maze. And that caused us to ask him a few questions."

Gil's mom gripped his dad's hand. Gil backed against the wall.

"Now, sit," said Bert, "and I'll tell you everything I know, which is less than we'll know tomorrow."

Bert paused while they took seats, then he cleared his voice. "You do remember how we encourage our employees to bring their kids to work if they should drop in over the weekends?"

Gil's dad nodded.

"During the time Carver Titus was working on a version of Octagon Map, Rocky was a frequent visitor. One morning, Carver left Rocky alone in his office. Rocky apparently rifled through Carver's Octagon Map folder and found a list of words. Rocky thought they might be passwords to allow him a sneak preview of the game. Carver came back in, stopped Rocky, and closed the folder." Bert reached over and straightened the nameplate on his desk. "But that didn't stop Rocky from trying those passwords every Saturday he visited. That's why he remembered them."

Bert cleared his throat. "That was about two years ago," he said. "Now, let's move to today. You can probably guess what happened. Rocky saw Octagon Map on one of the screens, thought those old passwords might have been meant for the Gollywhopper Games, and he tried them one more time."

"On his own?" asked Gil.

"On his own," Bert Golliwop said.

"Then what was all the coughing?" asked Gil. "Weren't those signals?"

"In the beginning they were, but in the end, Carver was trying to tell Rocky to stop. And that brings us to the reason why Carver wanted him to stop." Bert Golliwop stood, adjusted his suit jacket, and sat back down. "It appears I'm stalling because Carver gave us some other unexpected information today, and I need to tell you this despite the fact I don't know all the details yet."

"Do you mean . . ." Gil's dad said. "Those passwords? Was he . . ."

Bert Golliwop nodded. "About a month before your arrest, Charles, when you'd been chosen over him for that promotion? Remember we sent you to that conference in New York?"

"I remember."

"While you were there, Carver's computer crashed, or so he said, and he decided to use yours. Seems he figured out how to get into your system. He was snooping around, and he opened an e-mail asking you about our plans to restructure the five-million-dollar Octagon Fund."

"So Carver put two and two together?" said Gil's dad.

"That's right," Bert said. "He opened the link to the Octagon fund, tried the old passwords—we 'll need to find out how he got those passwords—and found himself in control of that five million dollars. He was still mad that you were promoted over him, so to appease his temper, he programmed the fund to send you that money as a very mean practical joke."

"A joke?" said Gil's dad.

Bert nodded. "He was about to confess when the police stormed in. Then he got scared."

Gil's dad sighed. "That's why he left."

"Apparently," said Bert, "he was afraid someone would come after him. And when no one ever did, I suppose he felt safe enough to bring his kid here and try to help him win to make up for the promotion he never got. Sometime between then and now, Rocky overheard him say you were innocent, but Rocky had no clue his father was the guilty party.

"And I'd love to talk more about this, but that's all I know. I do have one more thing to say." Bert Golliwop stopped to adjust his cuff links, then looked back up at Gil's dad. "Understand that everything I did was to protect this company. So while I don't regret any of my words or actions, I am sorry you had to go through this experience."

Gil looked at his dad's near-blank stare. His mom's tears streaming down her face. He doubled over, letting his own tears drop onto his shoes.

He wanted to be magically transported home without cameras, without interviews. He needed to be alone with his family. For a day, a week. Long enough to grasp everything that had happened and everything this would mean.

Bang! Bang!

Metal hitting wood. Old Man Golliwop's wheelchair. The old man barged into the office. "I bribed someone to tell me what is going on. So, Bert. How will you make this right?"

"I doubt I truly can," said Bert Golliwop.

"Cut the baloney. First you offer a public apology. Then you get this man back working for you at ten times his salary. And . . ."

Gil started laughing. It began as a tickle in his throat that moved into his gut and came out large and grand. And he infected everyone in the room.

When it felt like he was about to rip his belly wide open, he took in a gasp and laughed and laughed and finally got himself under control until he almost felt like crying again. He inhaled so he wouldn't, and with the back of his hand, he wiped laughter tears from his eyes. Grabbed a tissue from a box Bert Golliwop was passing around. Blew his nose. Looked at every person in the room. All with tissues to their eyes and noses.

He started laughing again. This time not so hard. But it felt good.

Old Man Golliwop wheeled his chair right up to Bert. "I ask you again, son. How will you make this right?"

"Charles?" Bert Golliwop said.

Gil's dad held up his hand like a stop sign. "Don't ask me to come back, Bert. I've moved on. But there is something you can do."

"If he asks it," said Old Man Golliwop, "you will do it."

Gil's dad went to the desk, picked up a pen, wrote something on a piece of paper, and slid it toward Bert Golliwop.

"'KidZillionaire,'" he read. "What's that?"

"New video game," said Gil's dad. "I've been working on it for more than a year. Computer version, too."

"You what?" Gil said, barely able to form the words.

"The story's written," he said. "The computer code's about a week from being complete. I have a design team working on the graphics right now. It's excellent. I guarantee. You'd save me the trouble of trying to sell it to Sony or Nintendo."

"Sold," said Old Man Golliwop.

"Dad!" Bert Golliwop shook his head. "It's not your—"

"Company. I know," said the old man. "But it was, and I still remember enough to know you'd be a fool to pass this up. So I say sold!"

Charles Goodson smiled. "I haven't set a price yet."

"They'll buy it," said the old man.

"We'll talk," said Bert. "What's the premise?"

Gil's dad laughed. "It's about a kid who ferrets out the evil president of a toy company, takes over the business, and becomes a zillionaire."

"And I'm the evil toy company president?"

"Oh, of course not," said Gil's dad.

"Right." Bert Golliwop smiled and stood. "When the dust settles, we'll talk anyway." He stuck out his hand. Gil's dad shook it. "Let's finish up this already long day," said Bert.

They filed from the office, Bert Golliwop pulling Gil to the lead with him. "I need to fill you in on what's been going on, and what will happen from here," he said. "We have Rocky and Carver Titus sequestered. The other three contestants have been reminded that they may not reveal anything about the Games or they'll forfeit their winnings plus pay the company and the TV network huge penalties. I know it will be harder for you, but you need to be a good actor for just thirty more hours, until the show has aired on both coasts. Then you're free to speak to anyone you want about anything you want. Understand so far?"

Gil nodded.

Mr. Golliwop pushed the ground-floor button inside the elevator. "When we get back, you'll sit down for your interview. And it will be all about you. Ready?"

Gil entered the victory room once again, and cameras flashed, TV cameras followed him. The network news anchor led him to a set of directors' chairs set up in a circle of spotlight. She interviewed him as if he were a celebrity. Question after question after question.

Soon Bianca bounded in. She pulled him up and spun him around. "I knew you could do it. I knew it. I knew it. I knew it!"

Lavinia and Thorn joined them. The cameras circled again, clicking and flashing and shooting so much footage, Gil wished he had a nickel for every— Wait. Now he did.

They posed and posed and spoke some more, and just after Bert Golliwop mentioned to Bianca that he might want her in some of his commercials, they finally headed out the door together, saying they'd IM and e-mail as soon as Gil could get back online.

Gil and his parents walked past the green arrows,

past the windup toys, and into the sun-drenched parking lot that was nearly as deserted as Bert Golliwop had promised. Had they really parked there just this morning? Or was that another boy in another lifetime?

"What's that?" said Gil's dad, pointing to the car.

On the trunk were five sticky notes, each with one word: TROVER PARK TOMORROW AT 4:00. The notes were arranged in the shape of an F. "Frankie," Gil said.

Gil collected them, smiled more, climbed inside the car.

He and his parents sat there, windows down, ignition off. No cameras. No microphones.

Gil leaned his head back, closed his eyes. Let out a laugh. He turned to his dad. "So. KidZillionaire. Why were you keeping it a secret?"

"It wasn't on purpose." His dad looped one hand over the steering wheel. "You saw me with those computer code books. All those files. I've been sitting in the open, at the dining room table, working on the game."

"I thought you were still looking for . . ."

"This whole time?" said his mom. "You thought he was poring over those detective files?"

Gil nodded.

His dad chuckled. "I haven't looked at those for months and months. Even before The Incident, I started fooling around with ideas for a video game. Sitting in jail that night, I came up with Kid-Zillionaire. Thinking about that took my mind off everything else that was happening."

"But the calls to the detectives . . ."

"Sure. At first I was trying to solve it, but one night I got so bored looking at the same files over and over, I jotted down my thoughts about that game. Within a week, I stopped looking at the trial files and started creating new files for this. And I suppose I was so used to working alone, I never talked about it." He turned on the ignition. "Besides, I didn't want to get your hopes up. It's hard to sell concepts like this."

Gil nodded again. And understood.

"You want to know the best part about this kind of work? I can do it anywhere in the world. So wherever you want to move . . ."

Wherever he wanted to move.

They pulled out of the parking lot, none of them saying a thing.

Wherever he wanted to move. He wanted to live in a place where he could be a normal kid with normal friends and a normal life.

Gil's interviewer had made that sound impossible. "You understand you'll be famous after tomorrow night," she'd said during the interview. "What will you do with your fame?"

"I just want to be a regular kid who had a really, really good day," he'd answered.

And how would he deal with people who wanted to hang around just because he'd won?

Gil thought he'd be able to sort out the good people from the fakers. Eventually.

But for now he had time to sit back and grin. In private. No one knew he won yet. They only knew he'd made it to the final ten. He wouldn't be anyone's winner until after the TV broadcast. For tonight and tomorrow, he was just Gil.

In a couple hours, they'd go out to dinner. Gil's

treat. Steaks. At the best restaurant. They'd slink out of the house. Unnoticed.

Or not. Even before their car turned the corner to their street, both sides of the road were lined with people. Holding signs.

"I don't want to look," said Gil.

"Why not?" said his dad.

"What if they're mad I made the final ten?"

"I wouldn't worry," said his mom. "Mad doesn't come with balloons."

The signs had balloons. The people had balloons. And as they passed, the people launched their balloons into the air.

"But they don't know if I won or lost. They don't know anything."

They pulled into the driveway to the claps and cheers of the crowd. Mrs. Hempstead, whose lawn had almost made him too late for this moment, rushed up with a cake. "You're our hero no matter how you did," she said, giving him a kiss on the cheek. "Now tell us how you did."

"Sorry, Mrs. Hempstead," Gil said, trying not

to smile too big. "They won't let me."

"Hey, Gil," came a voice from the crowd. "Over here! Gil! Catch!" Frankie lobbed a football over three rows of people.

The ball drifted back, back, sending Gil toward the side of the house, leaping over a small bush. Making the catch.

The crowd cheered.

"He's our new wide receiver!" Frankie yelled. "Right, Gil?"

Gil looked at his mom. Looked at his dad. Looked at Frankie.

A normal kid with normal friends.

Gil looked at his parents again. Pointed to a sign that said, WELCOME HOME.

He lobbed the ball back in the air. "You got it, Frankie."

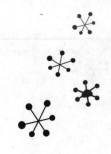

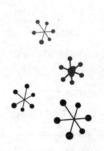

One More Puzzle

Gil double-clicked his mouse. Onscreen, the door opened. He was in the office of Ackrud Toy Company's Evil President. Before Ackrud Weevil ran out the back door, Gil clicked on the slip of paper attached to his shoe.

"Yeah!" he said. It was the last two letters of the grid. Finally. With all his travels for Golly this past summer, it had taken Gil a month to navigate to the last level of KidZillionaire—or at least the last level in this test version. Now he'd get the password to Ackrud's computer. Except . . .

"Dad, you're missing a word here."

Gil's dad got up from the other desk chair in their new upstairs office. "Huh?"

"Look. It reads, 'Start with a,'" he said. "Start with a duck? Start with a doughnut? Start with a what?"

His dad grew a sly smile. "Just solve the puzzle," he said, then left the room.

Gil shrugged, clicked through the building, back to the company's main computer. Fine. He'd type the letters in order.

No. Gil had learned his lesson from the Games. Those letters meant something. He sat there and stared.

O	M	I	C	S
T	I	T	K	T
A	M	E	N	I

Start with a

Start with a what? Start with a what? Start with a—

"Hey, Gil!"

"Upstairs, Frankie!"

Time for freshman football practice. This would have to wait. Again. Or . . . aha! Gil saw his way through that maze of letters. Seconds later, he knew what he needed to do. Watch out, Weevil! Soon the Ackrud Toy Company will be mine!

Gil grabbed his cleats. He'd figure out the password later.

HINTS:

* This is a maze of letters
* Figure out where to start
* Move vertically, horizontally, or diagonally
* Use each letter only once
* The letters will spell three words
* The words all can be used to modify the name of an object
* That object is your answer

ANSWER:

That night, when Gil typed in the answer, he set off a timer connected to the common object—a bomb (puzzle words + "bomb" = "atomic bomb," "stink bomb," "time bomb").

"If I can't keep this toy company," said the Evil President, "no one can."

It was now up to Gil to race onscreen around Ackrud and find out how to stop that bomb from exploding.

Acknowledgments

When it came time to write my acknowledgments, I decided to think about it as a competition. The only rule: Name each person whose support contributed to the publication of *The Gollywhopper Games*. No problem, I thought. I can name every one of those people in my sleep. Just watch.

Thanks go to Rebecca Davis, who brought this book to the table; to editors Steve Geck, Martha Mihalick, and Sarah Cloots, whose invaluable feedback kept me honest; and especially to my editor Virginia Duncan, who, with her quiet confidence, pushed me to get more from my characters and their story.

Also to art director Paul Zakris, to cover artist John Rocco, and to artist and designer Victoria Jamieson, whose vision and talents added a whole new dimension.

A huge amount of gratitude goes to my agent, Jennie Dunham, who believed in Gil as much as, and sometimes more than, I did.

I'm supremely grateful for my writing community. This is such a solitary business, I'd go bonkers if it weren't for the camaraderie and critiques of writers and authors Cindy Lord, Lynn Fazenbaker, Carol Norton, Tracy Hurley, Claudia Pearson, Barbara Ehrentreu, and the rest of the YA-Authors who have helped my writing grow; of Leslie Wyatt, who found me from across the state; of Kate Raybuck, Maggie Fowler, and Doris Mueller, who have read far too many versions; and of the YAckers2, whose direct fingerprints may not appear on this book but whose influences certainly do.

I can't forget Phillip Norfleet, my first fan, and Julia Bald, whose eye for detail is remarkable.

Much love and more thanks than I could ever give go to my friends and family for believing this would happen, for giving me space when it didn't, and celebrating with me when it did. Special mention goes to Debbie Poslosky, who supplies me with her boundless enthusiasm and an endless pool of young minds whenever I need them; to Bill and Carol Simon, who made books and art a steady part of my life; to Dick Feldman, who understood how important it was for me to try this; to Cassie Feldman, who kept me laughing and distracted when I needed it most; and to Paige Feldman, who has been my biggest supporter ever since she fell in love with Gil from the first draft, who never allowed me to get away with anything less than perfection, and who also vowed to produce *The Gollywhopper Games* if no one jumped on it before she was ready.

After I finished this part of the list, I realized I could never win the acknowledgments game. What about all the other editors who have no clue how much impact they've had on this book? What about the rest of the people I'll remember I forgot to mention once this is in print? And what about the student who returned *Charlie and the Chocolate Factory* to the school library one day when I was volunteering? He asked the librarian for another story like it, but neither she nor his teacher could find a title to satisfy him. It was at that moment I decided to write a book for that ten-year-old boy, and I will be forever indebted to him . . . whoever he is.